# BAD RHYTHM

THE WINSTON BROTHERS
BOOK THREE

DORI PULITANO

# Roland

THE SMELL of leather fills my senses as I listen to the sound of my own breath and wait in silence for her commands. Being here is dangerous for a man like me, but it doesn't stop me from donning the blindfold—or the bindings that keep my hands immobile behind me.

I jerk as the pointy tip of her high-heeled boot presses into my bare back. "Lean forward, Pet." The rasp of her voice makes my cock harden like a steel pipe, pressing against the fabric of my boxer briefs. Doing as she orders I heave myself over at a ninety-degree angle, careful not to fall on my face. "Such a good boy." The sole of her boot drags against my skin as if she's petting a dog. As quick as I obey, the unforgiving smack of her paddle lashes my backside, making my dick pulse with need. My underwear is wet from the pre-cum leaking from the tip. As she swats me again, I groan with desire.

"Does that feel good, *Pet*?" She leans down, her tongue dragging along my neck as the heat of her breath pauses by my ear. "You need to get off, Pet? Is your cock weeping with need?"

"Yes, Mistress," I grumble, knowing full well she won't do a damn thing about it.

That's not the relationship we have. She gives me the punishment I crave, but sex is not part of the deal. Instead, she'll call in another submissive to get me off. We've been at this for nearly an hour. My dick is hard as nails, and she knows it—especially now as her hand slides around my side and straight between my legs. This is a first for her, which has me tensing as her fingers slip beneath the elastic band of my boxer-briefs and around my cock.

"Mistress?" I whimper my question, confused at the sudden change in how we operate.

Her hand tightens around my throbbing rod. "Maybe I want a turn, Pet. I've watched as I get you hard as steel, then pass you off to someone else to enjoy the fruits of my labor. Does that bother you?" She squeezes me again.

"No Mistress. I just thought..." My voice falters as she jerks me in her palm.

"Roll over, Pet." She releases my bound arms with her free hand and nudges me to roll onto my back. Doing as she commands, I flop onto the floor, keeping my hands at my sides. "Good boy. Now... I will still give you your treat, but this time *I'm* going to play. I want your cock for myself."

My dick pulses in response. "Yes, Mistress. Whatever you want."

I hear the door open, then close, followed by the soft sound of feet padding across the floor. Soft hands press into my chest, as Mistress continues pumping my shaft. "Take off your panties." Mistress commands the visitor to kneel beside my head, making my body thrum with excitement. She's never taken part like this, and I swear to Christ I'm nearly ready to explode. "Sit on his face and let him eat your cunt, little mouse."

The visitor climbs over my head and positions her dripping wet cunt above me. I can't see her, but the musky scent of her pussy is like a drug for me. I gasp when Mistress tugs my boxers down below my hips and covers me with a condom. "Put your hands on her, Pet. I want to watch as you pleasure her with your tongue."

I lean forward slightly, swiping my tongue into her folds. She hisses at the contact, rocking her cunt against me. My body tenses and I nearly cum on the spot as Mistress slides down on my dick, burying me inside her warm pussy. "Fuck." I grunt, knowing full well the outburst will have a consequence.

When her fingers latch onto the nipple ring and twist, I wheeze at the sensation. It *should* cause pain. Instead, it's like a trigger for my cock and instead, I pulse inside her sweet cunt. "Pet." She mumbles above me. "Let go of her and fuck me like you own this cunt."

I release the girl above me, still eating her pussy with fervor, and latch onto Mistress's hips. Thrusting my body beneath her, I drive my shaft into her with such force the girl riding my face cries out as my teeth scrape against her most sensitive areas. Her sudden movement causes my blindfold to slip off and I glance up to find a masked woman above me. Her head is pressed into Mistress's as their tongues dance against each other. The sight drives me wild with need and I pound into Mistress like a wild beast.

"Stop." She presses her palms into me, halting my hips. I watch as she climbs off, holding her hand out to the woman I still have my tongue buried in, and pulls her to her feet. My cock weeps with the loss of her heat, but my eyes watch in rapt fascination as the mistress retrieves something from the dresser.

"Put this on." She hands the masked woman the strap-on dildo and helps her fasten it to her body.

My heart quickens inside my chest as I watch her guide her back over to me. I might like the pain she doles out and the occasional anal plug, but a strap-on that's new even for me. I'm not one to back down from a challenge, but I find my safe word on the tip of my tongue as I question her. "Mistress?"

"Don't worry, Pet. This is for me… not you."

She lies the woman on her back, adjusting the massive dildo and coating its rubbery exterior in lube. "Get up, Pet." She snaps her fingers at me, making me scramble to my knees. "I want you to fuck my ass as I ride her."

She hands me the bottle of lubricant, and I watch as she climbs on top of the dildo. She cries out, her body tensing as the rubber cock disappears inside her. Reaching behind herself, she fiddles with something until the unmistakable sound of the vibrator whirls to life. The masked woman cries out, the strap-on obviously hitting her clit as Mistress rides her.

"Pet." Mistress whimpers my name. Her breaths come out in short gasps as she leans over and presses her lips to the woman and bares her ass to me.

Adjusting the condom, ensuring it's still intact, I coat her hole with the gel liquid and toss the bottle to the floor. Gripping the globes of her ass, I line my shaft up with the tiny star and press inside. I bite my lower lip to not cry out. Between the sensation of her muscles gripping my cock and the vibration of the dildo buried inside her sweet cunt, I know I won't last.

"Mistress, may I move?" I plead, my voice cracking with desire.

"Yes, Pet." She moves against me, her body pulsing around my dick as I pull out and slam back in.

Topping her like this, I become the one in control. "Do you like this, Mistress? Do you like my cock buried inside your ass?"

She cranes her head, glancing over her shoulder, realizing the beast has come out to play. "Yes, Pet." Mistress whines as my cock assaults her from behind. I'm not a small man, so I recognize her ass is going to hurt tomorrow.

Our combined moans and the sound of skin on skin fill the space. Mistress tenses under my fingers and I watch in complete rapture as she cries out her release. The masked woman follows her into bliss and screams as her orgasm bursts free. I'm not far behind as my body stills behind Mistress and empties into the condom inside her ass. I sit back on my heels, my dick pulling free of her body and falling limp against my thighs. Mistress pushes to her feet and stalks from the room, leaving me and the mystery woman alone. For a moment, I stay frozen in my spot, but quickly snap out of my stupor and push to my feet. The condom clings loosely to my dick, the thin rubber filled with the evidence of my release. Carefully, I roll the barrier off and tie the end.

Not caring what the mystery woman is doing, I turn on a heel and stalk toward the attached bathroom. After tossing the rubber into the trash, I brace my hands against the sink and stare at my reflection. My life hasn't been all roses and sunshine and it's deeply affected me in ways nobody else would understand outside these walls. For whatever reason, I *need* the punishment to remind me where I come from.

Thank God no one knows this side of me. If they did, they'd call me a pervert. Keeping this hidden has been a challenge, but a necessary one. I can't imagine what would happen if it ever got out...

My life would be utterly *fucked*.

---

"I'm not doing it." I cross my arms across my chest and growl as I stare at the photo that Harold, my manager, slaps down on the glass surface in front of me. "I don't care *what* the label says. I'm not letting you turn me into some kind of fucking choir boy to save face. It's not who I am, nor will it *ever* be." I glare at the one person I wasn't expecting to see again--and to make matters worse, she's apparently being hired to clean up my reputation. At least that's what Harold is *trying* to explain to me in a way that doesn't put me on edge...and he's utterly failing.

"Roland." Harold's sigh and the slight shake of his head warns me I will not win this argument the way I intend. "That photo hurts your image—worse than last year's with Kai Townsend." He puffs out a frustrated breath at the mention of the super model I had been caught fucking from behind on camera. "And *your* image is the *label's* image. This isn't something they're going to sit back and allow to unfold as it may. We need Ms. Holiday to turn shit around. *You* need her to turn it around or the label is going to cut ties with you. Is that what you want? For your career to come to an abrupt halt because you're a public relations nightmare? Fuck, you're only twenty-five, Roland. You're in your prime."

I push the photograph away from me like it's going to bite my hand. "For fuck's sake, I'm hardly the first guy to be caught with his pants down. What I do in my own time with my own money is my own damn business. What about the bitch who leaked the fucking image? It's not like I *consented* to a documentary. Where are we on that?"

Harold groans as he gives me a look. "She's going to pay, but the damage is done. You know as well as I do that anything that *gets* out is out forever. There's no pretending it didn't happen. We're not exactly quashing rumors here, Roland."

I mull over his words and bristle at the fact he's right. The moment the tabloids got their dirty hands on that picture, my private life was no longer that. Now, it's a goddamn circus and I'm the freak in the center ring.

"It's not like it's the first time, either." The curt, blistering tone in Ms. Holiday's voice cuts through the tension, making my gaze snap in her direction. She's not the same girl I remember from school. Sure, she's still got the sprinkling of freckles across her nose and the same auburn red hair—but Isabella Holiday is even more beautiful all grown up. *And* from what I hear, one of the best at cleaning up celebrity fuck ups. Which is exactly what led to the face-to-face meeting after ghosting her years ago—she's here to fix what I broke. At least *some* things never change.

Narrowing my eyes at her, I lean forward. "So? I'll say it again... it's my *private* life."

"That may be true, Mr. Winston. But the fact remains, it's no longer a mystery to your fans what you do behind closed doors - and it destroys your carefully crafted image of availability that keeps them coming back for more."

Grunting, I cross my arms over my chest, "They *should* be interested in me as a performer and in my music."

She stares at me, pinning me with a look that says I'm walking on thin ice, "Oh, they certainly got a performance and let me tell you— that's not the show they want to see... *whatever* it is you were doing."

"Fucking—Ms. Holiday. Or should we cut the shit with the formali- ties—*Izzy?*" When my words detonate like a bomb, I can't hide the smirk as she stiffens. "I was *fucking.* Whether you want to address that aspect of this or not, sex keeps this world populated."

Quickly shaking off her shock, she locks her gaze with mine. "Sex or not, your reputation is not something you want to destroy. Not everyone understands your..." She clears her throat and adds, "... kink." She swallows, my eyes narrowing in on the bob of her throat. "They're calling you a pervert, Roland. Is that what you want to be known for?"

I sit back in my chair and close my eyelids. This is *exactly* what I was afraid of. Fortunately, they don't see just how much of a pervert I am, or this would be much worse. "I had a threesome. How is that perverted? It's like every red-blooded man's *dream...* and probably most women's, too."

"Really?" Izzy scoffs. "You were photographed with your cock buried inside one woman, while another paddled you from behind. People find that trashy."

Moving around the table, I press my face close to hers as my teeth clench and my voice lowers to a growl. "Do *you?*"

"Do I what?"

"Find it trashy." I watch as her eyes dilate at my words. "You didn't think lowly of me when we were in school."

She blinks as her tongue swipes at her bottom lip. "It doesn't matter what I think. *My* sexual preferences aren't the ones on trial in the media." She leans back and blows out her frustrated breath. "And that was nearly ten years ago. A lot can happen in that amount of time. People change, Roland. Things *change* people. But I'm not the one risking my career. *You* are. Either you want my help or not."

I scoff at her callous words. Even though I know she's right, I still can't admit to myself I fucked up. "What would your services entail?" Leaning back in my chair, I cross my arms over my chest and cock an eyebrow at her.

Harold clears his throat, breaking the Mexican standoff we're having with our locked gazes. "Roland, what her duties entail doesn't matter. You don't really get a say in this. The label hired her, so she's staying and you're going to have to work together to get these media shitstorms under control - or you can find a new label." Harold pushes up from the table and pauses. "Take some time to work out the details. And since it seems you two already know each other, maybe this won't be as bad as you think, Roland. I look forward to working with you, Ms. Holiday." He moves around the long glass top and pauses when he reaches the door. "Oh… and Ms. Holiday?"

She glances over at him. "Yes?"

"Good luck." He cuts me a knowing smirk. "You're going to need it."

The silence is deafening as Harold shuts the door, leaving Izzy and me alone. "Well… let's get this over with. I have more important shit to do." I grumble the last part at her, turning from the vacant spot Harold just left.

"Tell me something." I watch as she leans forward, her eyes narrowing to me. "Does it bother you that the world knows what kind of sexual encounter gives you satisfaction?"

My chair moves back as I push to my feet and lean across the smooth surface. Izzy presses her back against the chair as I invade her space. "I get my satisfaction in many ways, *Miss* Holiday. If you'd like me to show you just how I like to have my cock stroked, all you have to do is ask. It'd be just like old times."

Her sharp intake of breath makes me smirk. "I have no interest in anything related to your cock ever again, *Mr.* Winston."

Raking my eyes over her tense frame, I note how the vein in her throat pulses—not to mention the way her pupils dilate from my crass words. "You can say whatever you want, Izzy. Though, I can almost bet you're clenching your thighs together to quell the pulsing need humming between them. But don't worry—you're not my type anymore, sweetheart." I straighten my back and start toward the hallway. "Call me when you figure out how to 'clean' my —" I make air quotes with my fingers. "…image up."

I leave her sitting at the conference table and stomp my way to the elevator. Liam, my long-time bodyguard, leaned against the wall, waiting for me. The anger burning in my chest leaves me feeling confused beyond measure because I can't decide if I'm pissed she's here to clean up my image... or if it's because she didn't seem the least bit interested in me. Once upon a time, Isabella Holiday was the girl I thought I'd marry. But I was seventeen and stupid. After getting my big break in music my senior year—she and I went our separate ways... or more like I left her for the bright lights of Nashville.

Either way, she's here like a seance has resurrected her ghost from my past. Isabella Holiday is going to cause me more than a headache... she's going to cause heartache—and *that* has me scared shitless.

# 1

Izzy

THIS MAN IS GOING to kill me. I'm sure of it. Six *long* weeks and with every step I get closer to cleaning up his reputation, he sets us back three. And I won't lie—he's the epitome of All-American with good looks and ample charm - and even more now that he's a man. But his reckless behavior and questionable personal life make him seem *sleazy*. Which is where I come in. I'm one of the best in the Atlanta area at cleaning up train wrecks left behind by people with more money than sense. It honestly came as no surprise when my boss dropped music superstar Roland Winston's file on my desk after seeing the media coverage of his latest fling. Of course, I told him I'd take the contract… too bad I left out one tiny detail the day I agreed to help him. Okay, it was a *huge* one, but not something my boss needed to be made aware of.

*"Izzy, I need you to fly to Nashville and clean this fucking disaster up."*

*I pick up the manilla folder and flip it open. Staring back at me are the lewd photos of the music icon and boy I once knew—intimately. My heart stutters inside my chest as I stare at the compromising position Roland is photographed in and wonder what happened to the boy I once thought I loved.*

*"Wow… he's into some interesting stuff, I see."*

*Alan snorts. "You could say that, but that's neither here nor there. The shitty part is someone leaked the photos and now his label is unglued over it. The good news? A friend of mine over there reached out and asked for my best PR person at any cost. That's you, Izzy."*

I should've argued with Alan and found a way out of this. But now, a month and a half later, I'm questioning both my ability *and* sanity. Especially considering that photo was only the beginning. I blow out a frustrated breath as I stare at the newest leaked picture I received via email. And if I thought the first was bad, this one is… well—bad doesn't begin to cover it. Leaning back in my chair, I toss the kinky display of sexual gratification onto my desk and close my eyes. How in the hell am I supposed to make Roland into what the label wants when he's constantly doing shit like this? I swear the man is intentionally sabotaging his career. The sound of my door creaking open alerts me he's finally answered my summons. For a month, I've wanted to either claw out his eyes or rip off his clothes. And neither option would solve anything.

"You called for me?" Roland's sultry voice causes yet another unwanted reaction from my body. And it's one I've beaten myself up for over the last few weeks. My skin pebbles when he walks into a room, and that has me pissed *and* confused. I crack open my eyes to find Roland throwing himself into the chair across from me dramatically. His head of security, Liam, stands in the corner watching our interaction with something that resembles a hybrid between a smirk and a scowl. It's almost like he knows how this is going to go down before it happens and that sets my nerves on-edge.

I sit up and push the photo in his direction, desperately trying to conceal my disgust with him. "Care to explain *this*?"

Liam muffles a snort as Roland fingers the picture, never lifting it from the wooden surface. "*Fuck.*"

"Yeah, thank you Captain Obvious."

I glare at him like I have every intention of reaching across the desk to pop him upside the head, but instead, I inhale and exhale slowly, trying to control my temper. "What the hell? You promised me you'd keep this shit on the down low. And this—"

I sigh, the tension in my neck causing the telltale sign of a headache threatening to emerge. "...is anything but! I don't even know what to say. The last set of leaked images was you in a ménage. But this? This is something entirely different. I get it, okay? People have their... things... and—" I trail off as I avoid looking at the photo that he's spinning around underneath his finger. I *don't* really get it, but it's not my place to judge. My job is to salvage his career—which is quickly going up in flames. "You're into... some weird stuff. But the public should never know about it."

Roland leans back, his arms fold across his chest as he cocks an eyebrow at me. "Weird stuff?"

I furrow my brows as my face scrunches in disgust. "Yeah, Roland. Weird. That..." I stab my finger into the image. "...is not considered normal to most people. *I'm* not judging you, but you must recognize this isn't what people expect when they see photos of you. I'm curious... are you not able to have a traditional relationship with a woman anymore? I mean, I don't remember you being like this when we were kids. You certainly weren't when *we* dated."

I can't help myself. I need to understand if he's just incapable of a normal sexual relationship with the opposite sex anymore. Of course, staring at the image of him bound and blindfolded, I can't help but feel somewhat turned on by it, but I shove that feeling aside as I look away. Roland leans across the table, putting himself closer to me.

"Some people like to spice up their sex, Isabella. But I'm going to assume by your ignorant remark you're still a missionary kind of woman." He snaps back, shoving his chair as he stands. "Not everyone loves vanilla, and you need to back off the kink-shaming. The only question right now is, how are you going to spin this for me?"

The snort escapes before I realize it. "Sorry... but do you seriously think I can fix this if you're not willing to change?"

A knock interrupts us, and I stand, moving around him toward the door. "I'm starting to think you don't *want* your image cleaned up." Pulling open the door, I sigh when I see who's standing on the other side. "Harold. How *kind* of you to join us." I step aside and wave him into the room. "Maybe you can explain to our resident rockstar how I'm a public relations specialist—*not* a miracle worker and that these continued images are going to be his downfall."

"Roland." Harold grumbles his name as I pull the office door shut, his entire posture turning defensive the moment their gazes meet. "Boy... you're determined to sabotage yourself, aren't you?"

"That wasn't my intention, no. You're acting like I *hired* whoever is taking these to do this. I'm as surprised as you are. Why can't people just leave me the fuck alone? Aren't I allowed to have a private life?"

I grind my teeth in frustration. A part of me feels sorry for him— the other wants to turn him over my knee and punish him for being so irresponsible. "Sure. If it was actually *private*. But it's not, and that's why we're here right now. If this was your longtime girl- friend, then the person leaking the images would be the bad guy for invading your privacy. But she's clearly not. You were photographed a few months ago in a ménage à trois with *different* women. It's hard to accuse someone of invading your privacy when you're doing nothing to protect it."

"That's it!" Harold snaps his fingers, the grin on his face making me cringe. "You need a girlfriend."

"No." Roland plops down in the chair as he shakes his head. "I don't have time for a girlfriend."

"Not a real one, Roland. But a fake one for the press. And you—" he points at me. "…are the perfect person to play that role."

"Me?" I narrow my gaze at him. "No fucking way. I was hired to clean up his image, not play a doting girlfriend or babysitter. Been there… done that, got the broken heart as a souvenir. There is no way in hell I'd ever be seen with him in that capacity now."

Harold stares at me a whole breath before dropping into a persuasive tone, "You were hired to fix this mess. And you, yourself, just said a girlfriend would do the trick. We can't risk someone else getting involved and leaking the ploy to the public. Plus, you've already signed an NDA."

"No." Roland glares at me. "No one on this *planet* would believe I'd date someone like her nowadays."

I gasp at his callous words. "Well, the feeling is mutual. And dating you is the last thing I'd ever agree to again." Fisting the doorknob, I jerk open the door. "This conversation is over. I don't give a fuck if it gets me fired and I lose *everything*. Being your fake girlfriend to help you out of the media shitstorm you created will never happen. Now, if you'll excuse me, I need to call my boss. I don't think me being your PR representative is going to work out any longer."

The rage I'm feeling is barely containable as I stab my finger into the elevator button. A fake girlfriend is the last thing that a self-absorbed rockstar needs—what he *needs* is a therapist. Roland Winston might be good-looking, but he has some deep-seated issues I can't fix. Slipping inside the metal box, I lean my back against the cool metal wall and close my eyes. As I step out to leave, I roll my eyes as Roland steps out from the second elevator and bee lines straight for me.

"Izzy, *wait.*" He calls out behind me, but I ignore him, refusing to rehash the conversation.

I hear him calling me as he tries to catch up, but I spot the company car waiting for me and climb inside, slamming the door closed. When I finally work up the courage, I glance toward the front of the building and see him standing on the sidewalk with his hands in his pockets. His face looks bewildered, almost regretfully, as the car pulls into traffic.

"Where to, ma'am?"

Realizing I haven't spoken a word to the driver, I blink back tears and speak. "Take me to Breakstone Heights, please."

He nods, knowing my apartment is owned and provided by Roland. To my dissatisfaction, I wasn't given much choice about where I would stay during my time with the label here in Nashville. The driver's eyes watch me a little longer in the rearview mirror before he finally speaks.

"You okay, Miss Holiday?"

"Yes." I force out the words in a whisper, exhaustion from this entire clusterfuck threatening to pull me under any minute. My emotions waver between wanting to choke him—or kiss him just so I can see if he's the boy I once knew underneath this bullshit image he's built.

As soon as the car pulls into the circular drive of my temporary home, I thank my chauffeur and head into the lobby. The building is beautiful, and probably more than I could afford on my normal salary—but everything comes with a price, and mine is dealing with the pompous prick Roland Winston.

I've barely shoved my key in the lock when I hear him.

"I didn't take you as a coward."

Glancing over my shoulder, I let my eyes roam over him. His head is tilted, and his eyes burn into me like they have the power of a thousand suns. If you've ever heard the saying wish in one hand and shit in another... you can guess which hand is currently hot. My wish just evaporated into a steaming pile of poo.

"Why are you here, Roland? It's pretty apparent to me you have no desire to fix your image, which means you're making it impossible for me to help you."

Roland steps forward and presses his palms against my door, caging me between it and him. "I think you lied back there because I hurt your feelings."

The snort escapes before I can stop it. "Hurt my feelings... Do you even *hear* yourself? You think this is about *feelings*?"

He leans in, closing the gap between our bodies even more. "Isn't it, though? You can lie to yourself, but I see you aren't disgusted by me, *Izzy*." His knee wedges between my legs, pressing dangerously close against my core. One that's tingling with betrayal, despite hating him with every fiber of my being. "In fact, I think seeing me in those pictures like that turns you on."

"You're wrong." My words come out breathless, and I notice the slight smirk in his expression when I look into his eyes. "I despise you."

# 2

Izzy

"Then what would you have to lose by pretending to be my girlfriend for a little while? It wouldn't be that difficult, seeing as we've done that whole song and dance before."

"Aside from my *dignity*? Unlike you, I have a reputation I am *proud* of and don't plan to sully it by being seen with *you*." I chuckle at my own words. "Besides, you're right... no one would believe it. I'm obviously not your type and even if I *was*, it's been years since we were together, and I *still* hate you."

He moves his leg, brushing his knee on my overly sensitive center. "I think you *want* to hate me, but deep down," his hot breath burns against my ear as he leans in close. "...you wonder what it would be like to have my cock buried between your wet folds again."

My breath hitches as I shake my head in refusal, silently trying to deny his words. Even if there's any chance they're true—I won't let Roland know that. Hell... he doesn't even know I thought we'd get married. I was certain we were on the highway towards *forever*... but like most speeding cars, you're always at risk for a wreck. And our relationship didn't just crash—it exploded and left my heart blackened and charred. Now, being here with him after all this time, I see nothing but more turmoil on the horizon.

"You should back up. Someone might see you like this and then we'll have one more rumor on your hands. Where the hell is Liam?" Glancing around for the massive man, I press my palms against his chest and give him a push. Digging my keys out of my bag, I turn my back to him and shove the door open, and stumble inside.

"I sent him away." Roland slips in behind me despite me trying to slam the door in his face. He kicks the door shut with his foot, continuing to follow me through the foyer. "I'll leave if you can honestly tell me you're not wet right now, thinking about my cock plunging into your slick cunt."

"Go home, Roland." I call out over my shoulder, making my way into the kitchen and leaning on the counter.

Roland grabs my arm, spinning me around so I'm facing him. He runs his hand down my side and cups my ass, giving it a squeeze. "I can already tell you're wet for me. And *you* know I'm not wrong. People wouldn't believe someone as innocent as you would be mine these days… but Harold's right—you might be the only person who can save my career."

"You're delusional, Roland—on so many levels. But you're right about one thing—I can save your career if you'd let me do my job and listen to me."

His fingers dig into my backside as he shifts closer. "Let go for a minute, Izzy. See how good we could be if you'd just give his idea a chance."

"No." I flatten my palms against his chest. "Not. Going. To. Happen."

He slips a hand around my front, edging the hem of my skirt up. My eyes widen as his fingers dance across my thigh. "Roland…" I grab hold of his hand, stilling the movement. "We need to keep this professional."

He slams his lips over mine. I gasp, giving him the access, he needs to slip his tongue inside. Heat burns through my body as I melt into him, giving just as much as he's taking. The kiss becomes demanding as he pushes against my body. The evidence of his arousal presses into my belly, making my own body respond in kind.

"Fuck." I gasp against his mouth as he pushes his fingers beneath my panties and brushes them across the red curls covering my mound.

"I *knew* it—you're soaked. You act like you don't want this, but you're nothing but a liar. You didn't use to be this uptight, Izzy. Don't you remember? There was a time you couldn't get enough of *us*."

"Roland…" I want to tell him to stop, but it feels too good. Every swipe of his fingers across my clit has my head spinning. "Oh, *God.*"

My eyes blink rapidly as my hands claw at the surface behind me, as if his very touch is literally going to drive me up the wall. When he plunges a single finger inside of my wetness, my breath stutters as he pushes until his hand is flush against my body, his thumb circling my clit as I squirm against his hand. He pumps his finger in and out of me as I struggle to focus, soft sounds of satisfaction slipping between my lips.

"Damn, Freckles. This is what I remember—the same warm, wet pussy begging for more. Fuck, you feel so good."

Like a bucket of cold water being dumped over my head, the memory of how he left me, severing my heart in two, hits me hard. Grabbing his hand, I jerk it out from between my legs. "But you're not the same guy I knew. You're the one being told what to do—the one being *bossed around.*" Roland's eyes bore into mine, searching for the lie I'm hiding. "You need to go. I won't do this with you—I can't."

He moves to step closer, but I let go of his hand and shove against him, trying to put space between us as he pleads with me, his voice twisting my insides. "Please, Izzy."

Shaking my head as I shove against the solid muscle wall of his chest with both hands, I try to keep my voice steady, even though my heart is racing inside my chest. "No, Roland. Go home and let me do my job."

He cups my cheek, holding my gaze as he ignores my attempts to put space between us. "What are you scared of Freckles?"

"Don't call me that—you lost that right a long time ago. Now move." I push him again, but when he doesn't budge, I wrap my hands around his neck as far as they will go, my thumbs sinking into the base of his throat as his eyes go wide with surprise. "Roland.. go...."

Practically choking him as I manhandle him backwards, I summon all of my strength to switch our positions until his back slams into the wall and I've seemingly got the upper hand. "I won't ask you again. What we just did was a slip in judgment. It won't happen again. You broke me once... you won't do it twice."

He makes a noise somewhere between a moan and a grunt as he straightens against the wall. "Jesus Christ." He mumbles, and I watch as I swear his pupils dilate. His eyes flick toward his feet as he mutters something I can't understand, but I shake my head and point to the door.

"I'll see you tomorrow, Roland." He needs to go before he sees the jacked-up feelings I know are scrawled all over my face. I'm caught between that feeling of love and hate—and wanting to finish what he started. My mind is so completely ablaze with the aftershock of nearly getting off on his fingers that I only vaguely hear the door opening and closing, signaling his retreat.

The betrayal of feelings coursing through my body makes me feel like I've made a huge mistake. Because *it* wants the pleasure of what his fingers promised even if it means he'd decimate my heart again. It's like a repeat of senior year when his music became more important than us. Just like history repeating itself—him getting what he wanted was more important than my feelings.

But even with the burning tendrils he left behind from his touch, hate bubbles underneath. My hip aches where he left his mark on my flesh, but worse, my pussy throbs from the feel of his fingers touching me. Repulsion should be the only thing I feel right now, but as I make my feet move and head toward the bathroom where I'll scrub away the memory of how he felt, a tiny part of me wants him to do it again... and *not* stop until I'm weak in the knees.

And *that* makes everything fucked up.

Because Roland is clearly not the boy from my past.

I flick on the shower and strip off my clothes. Stepping beneath the scalding water, I fill my loofah with body wash, desperate to wash away the sins of today. I scrub my body, praying for the memory of him to vanish. As the soapy scrubber brushes across the curls between my legs, Roland's face pops into my head. I'm borrowing trouble by letting him invade my thoughts like this because Roland can never know the conflicted truth buried in my heart. Once I rinse away all the reminders of the rock star's touch, I step out and brace myself against the sink. Wiping down the mirror, I stare at my reflection. The woman staring back is not the one from yesterday. This version of me is less confident, confused—and, well scared shitless.

Wrapping a towel around my naked body, I amble to my bedroom. My appetite is gone, so dinner is a bust. The only thing I want to do is climb into bed and forget about Roland Winston. I need to shove him back into the distant past where he belongs. Letting him infiltrate my present will only lead to disaster.

First thing in the morning, I'll resign from my position. Being around Roland will only cause me pain—pain I thought I'd left behind all those years ago. Back when he made it clear that the call of the neon lights of this godforsaken place meant more to him than I ever would.

I can't stay here. I don't care if it means running away with my tail between my legs—I need to leave behind this shitty town and all its fucked-up parts—especially *Roland.*

## 3

# *Roland*

THE AMBER liquid burns in my throat as I swallow the last of the whiskey and stare out into the night sky. I fucked up. *Big* this time. I let my attraction to a woman from my past, a woman meant to help my image, get the better of me and push me to do something stupid. A half-hearted laugh escapes my lips as I set down the empty tumbler.

*Stupid*.

That's laughable.

It's more like a momentous screw up. Despite the way her body responded to me, Izzy's not the same girl. Lifting my phone off the edge of the armchair, I stare at the darkened screen. I should call her—explain how I'm more fucked up than she realizes. I don't think she knows what really happened in her apartment—how wrapping her fingers around my throat like she was going to choke me made me cum in my pants like a prepubescent teenage boy.

But damn it, that's exactly what happened.

My dick stirs to life with the memory of her forcefully pushing me against the wall—the way her fingers dug into my skin as she demanded I leave. I can't shake the guilt coiling inside me at my reaction.

Is this the man I've become?

A man who can't get off without someone dominating me? I close my eyes as my palm squeezes around the frame of my phone, threatening to crack the glass. My therapist says this is all because of my childhood trauma. If only he knew the truth in his words— which he doesn't.

No one does.

Not even Gage or Drake know the truth of how much I saw... not of what I endured as a small child. They think seeing my monster of a father dead on the ground with a bullet hole in his chest was awful... if they only knew it's mild to the things that torment my nightmares.

Shaking myself from a trip down haunted lane, I swipe at the screen and wake it from its slumber. Thumbing through my contacts, I hover over Izzy's number. The simple icon stares back, mocking me like an evil omen. Taking a formidable breath, one that does nothing to still the nerves now burning through my veins, I press down on the screen. I don't expect her to answer, but her voice is like a strange melody—no like a siren's song luring the unaware ship's captain to his death.

"What do you want, Mister *Winston?*" Her tone tells me what I already know—she's pissed. "Have you decided to grow up and listen to me?"

I pause, searching for the words to say. I should tell her the truth. That would be the right thing to do. But instead, I choose what's comfortable. I bury it and let the bitterness swirling deep inside my heart take over, and the asshole persona I've created for myself slip out instead.

"Hardly, Freckles. I'm calling to see if you've given any more thought to the proposal, Harold suggested."

Her scoff is laced with a bitter undertone that's like a punch to my gut. "Are you fucking serious? The only thing I *plan* to do is tell him I quit. I want nothing to do with you or your fucked up life, Roland. You're not the boy I remember—you're something... darker."

My involuntary wince causes me to fumble with my phone and nearly drop it. Shifting in the chair, I grab the device and shove it against my face. "You wouldn't be the first to say that."

Her voice is resolute as she retorts, "And this won't be the first time you choose to ignore it either, I'm guessing?"

Pinching the bridge of my nose, I say words I instantly regret, though it's too late to take them back now. "Or the first time you run away from something because you're *scared*. People will talk and I'm sure the tabloids would love to make it into something more than it is. That does neither of our reputations any good. I think you should reconsider your plan, Freckles—for both our sakes."

"Are you fucking serious?" I can hear the rustling of her movement, making me realize she was likely in bed. "Wow—just wow." She grumbles to herself. "What happened to the boy I knew? I know you had a fucked-up childhood, but you didn't use to be like *this*."

Bitterly, I respond, "Or maybe you just didn't see that I've always been a lost cause."

Izzy groans through the phone. "Seriously, Roland. Can you see how fucked up what you're doing is? You have a problem. Sure, I won't lie and say for a minute I didn't get caught up in it... but it was a mistake. One that would jeopardize what we're trying to accomplish. Remember—clean up your career."

I straighten into a seated position against the plush cushion of the armchair at her admission. "Can you really call it a mistake, Izzy? I felt how your body responded to my touch. You wanted more…"

"Are you even listening to me? Or yourself, for that matter? You're demanding I stay on as your public relations manager, yet you *refuse* to acknowledge me and admit you have deeper issues…and feelings…"

I stiffen at her words. Izzy has always been able to see the truth, no matter how hard I try to mask it. Lashing out because it's the only thing I know how to do. "Stop right there, Izzy. Nobody said anything about feelings. This is business. Name your price and it's yours. It's a win for the both of us. I get my image cleaned up and you get a shit ton of money."

She snorts. "Not everything is about money, Roland. Sometimes it's about pride."

Pride is a funny thing. It's the one emotion that is supposed to drive you to be better—to do better. Only, the example I grew up with was something twisted beyond recognition.

Something *mangled* by darkness.

*Pride* cost my mother her life.

*Pride* made my father an abuser.

*Pride* means *nothing* to me.

"That word is meaningless. I don't give a shit about *pride*. There are only two things I care about in this life—music and my brothers. Beyond that, I don't give a fuck as to the *why* someone does something. I don't want your reasons. Either you risk leaving and ruining your career… or figure out how to fix my image and save yours in the process."

"Yeah... I know. Music has always been more important. I won't pretend to be your girlfriend, not even for all the oil in Saudi Arabia. But follow my guidance and I'll clean your image up—that's it, Roland."

"Fine." I grumble my response. I'll take what I get because as sick as it is... something about Izzy makes my body feel like I've laid hands on a live wire.

Her voice is stern as she adds, "And... what happened in my apartment will never be spoken about *or* happen again."

"Alright." I lean back and prop my feet up on the coffee table. "What's your great plan to make my image G- rated again?"

Izzy chuckles through the phone, the sound maniacal. "You will never be G-rated, Roland. But meet me tomorrow at the studio at nine. We'll talk then. And Roland."

"Yeah."

"If you ever touch me again, I'll *bite* off your cock. Are we clear?"

Sitting upright, the words tumble out before I can help myself. "Promise?"

Izzy groans on the other end and scolds, "Roland!"

I frown as I shove one hand against my throbbing dick, willing it to stay out of the conversation, even though her berating me has it standing at attention. "Crystal."

The silence that follows is a cold, stark reminder of the shitstorm likely waiting to explode from the circus I call my life. I'm not entirely sure why she's agreed to stay on. Funny thing is, she could have me by the balls if she wanted. She could *own* me if there wasn't hesitancy on her part and I better thank my lucky stars she's agreed not to quit and leave me explaining to the label why.

Needing a reminder of why I shouldn't allow the darkness to take hold, I swipe the screen again. The voice that answers is one of the two people who can calm my nerves.

"Roland... what's wrong?"

Gage's deep voice resonates through the line like a warm reminder of what's good in my life. "Why does anything have to be wrong for me to call my big brother?"

His baritone laugh makes me smile. "It's..." Gage pauses briefly, "After midnight. Why in the hell are you still awake? Shouldn't you be getting your beauty rest or something? I'd hate for your fans to see you worn out and looking less than the master behind Savage Realm."

"Har. Har. You're quite the comedian. Nah... I just missed hearing your old voice."

A sound in the background echoes through the line. "Shit, Rol. I gotta go. You sure you're, okay?"

"Yeah. Fine. Go save the world, big brother."

"Love you, Roland."

"Love you too."

I press the button and toss the useless device onto the table, leaning my head back onto the edge of the chair. There's only one other thing that's going to help me get my head out of the spiral it's in—music.

Pushing myself to my feet, I amble across the floor of my penthouse, stopping at the liquor cabinet to grab the bottle of whiskey beckoning me. Fisting the amber liquid in my hand, I settle myself in front of the piano. While I mainly play the guitar while singing, the piano is my first real love. Even if my record label doesn't see it fitting with the brand they've created, I'll never stop playing. Especially in times where my anxiety is threatening to create catastrophic events—things I wouldn't be able to come back from. Tipping the glass bottle to my lips, I swallow the devil's courage and relish in the burn as it coats my throat.

Pushing the cover open, I settle my fingers along the ivory keys. The smooth surface of black and white is like Xanax for my soul as it renders the nervous beats of anxiety defenseless inside me. Grabbing my notebook and pen, I slide it open and begin toying with notes. It doesn't take long before words start pouring out.

*If you wanted my truth, then all you needed to do was ask.*

*It's pain I feel, so this can't be real.*

*I was never meant for love; it was never meant for me.*

*It was just one kiss, it was just one touch.*

THE SMOOTH TASTE of Whiskey is bitter on my tongue as I tap out the rhythm in my head, matching the sound with the strike of a key. Each pull of the bottle drags more pain to the surface, the words I'm ruminating on flowing like the poison burning inside me.

ANOTHER DRINK, another few lines.

*Love shouldn't hurt*

*Love shouldn't break*

*It's more than a feeling.*

*There's more that's at stake.*

*It's only one moment, one chance with fate.*

*You should've come with a warning*

I SNORT AT THE WORDS, the meaning far more than just a song. One more tug of liquid courage, another turn of phrase.

*Or maybe that was me.*

*Love shouldn't hurt*

*Love shouldn't break*

*It's more than a feeling.*

*There's more that's at stake.*

I toss my pencil to the top of the piano and read over my words. My heart beats wildly as my eyes start to lose focus. Every word I've written is the truth I'm afraid to face. Draining what little is left in my bottle of Jack, I slam the decanter on top of the baby grand. As I push to stand, my legs wobble and I fall to my ass onto the bench as the alcohol hits me harder than I expect. Taking a deep breath, I lay my head down, the clang of the keys sounding throughout the room. Sleep is the last thing I want to do, knowing the nightmares are waiting for me to visit, but the swirling of my senses over-powers me—and I close my eyes.

Even in my drunken slumber, I'm transported back to a time I wish never existed.

*"Are you sure that bastard is even mine?"*

*I cower behind the edge of the door, watching as my father berates my mother for the hundredth time. Drake and Gage think they've sheltered me, but they don't know what I see... what I hear. "Calvin... don't say that. Of course, he's yours. Each of the boys belongs to you—even if they aren't mine. I can't help your disgusting ways."*

*My mother turns toward me as she realizes I'm in the corner watching. Her movement makes my father catch sight, making his head turn toward me. "Look, the little bastard wants to watch."*

*"Watch what? What are you talking about, Calvin?"*

*She doesn't see it coming. But I do—I try to cry out. But he's much faster, throwing her to the bed. "Stand there, boy. Don't. Move.."*

*I stand frozen, as the monster I call dad wraps his fingers around my arm in a death grip and tugs me closer to the edge of the bed. "Watch what happens to your mom when she doesn't listen."*

*He lets go of me long enough to pull her to the edge of the bed. "Calvin. Please don't do this. Not in front of him. Please."*

*His backhand is almost as punishing as his fist as he strikes her. "Shut up."*

*He unzips his pants and I watch as rips her nightgown, and then plunges into my mother with an unforgiving thrust. My mother cries out, and although I'm only four, I know her whimpers are not ones of happiness. He continues his punishment on her, punishment his sick mind sees as pleasure. I don't know why exactly… I just know this is my fault. He doesn't want me, and she pays the price. A price I'll never be able to repay.*

*"What the fuck?" Gage's voice echoes through the ostentatious room. My eyes scan the ridiculous art plastered on the walls, trying to find something other than the disgusting display I'm being forced to watch. "Roland, come here." His firm hand grips my shoulder, leading me from the room. "You're a sick fuck, Calvin. I hope you rot in hell."*

*It's not the first time I've heard him call our dad by his name. Gage slams the door, cutting off the terror my father inflicts on the woman who is supposed to protect me. The woman who brought me into this hell she calls life.*

*"It's going to be okay, Roland. I promise you, buddy."*

*I nod mindlessly as he leads me into Drake's room. "Stay here with him." Gage shoves me toward Drake, turning back out of the room. "Dad—" he shakes his head in disgust. "Just watch him, ok?"*

*Drake takes me over to the bed and settles me on it. "Here, buddy, put these on. Music will drown out the noise."*

*I let the music wash out the screams, but it's too late.*

*The memories are burned inside me forever.*

## 4

Izzy

I'VE GOT to be the dumbest woman on the face of the earth. That's the only reason I can come up with as to why I'm sitting here waiting for a man who could essentially ruin me again. My fingernails drum across the surface of the table as I watch the door, waiting for Roland to appear.

Roland is not the same seventeen-year-old boy I remember from school. He's sexier, sure. But he's filled with a deep sadness and a barely veiled darkness that scares me. I'm surprised I beat him to the studio, seeing how it's his home away from home. Glancing down at my watch, I sigh, realizing he's officially fifteen minutes late. Just as I pull out my phone to call him, he strolls in.

"You're late." My eyes track his movement as he shuffles to the chair opposite me and drops his body into it like a sack of potatoes. I can't help but notice the dark circles around his eyes and the disheveled way his hair scatters across his face. Either he drank himself silly last night or nightmares kept him from getting rest. Or maybe *both*. "Jesus. Did you even sleep?"

"Can we just get this over with? Not everyone sleeps as perfectly as you, *Izzy*."

My eyes blink rapidly in irritation at his callous retort. As I open my mouth to snap back, I really look at him. The sorrow that radiates from his eyes that barely fill with light hits me square in the chest. Flicking my eyes to Liam, he shrugs his shoulders. He's probably the only other person who might know what's going on with him, and he looks just as confused.

"Hey… Rols." His head snaps up at the nickname I used when we were kids. The cerulean orbs track me as I get up and move to sit beside him. Reaching out, I take his hand in mine. "If I'm going to help you, I need to know what goes on inside here." I tap on his head. "Talk to me, please?"

For a millisecond, I see a flicker of the boy I remember. But the emotion is gone in a blink as his eyes seem to glaze over with the wall he's developed as a shield. Roland leans into me and presses his lips to my ear. "I was up tugging on my cock thinking of that *Tight. Hot. Pussy* I wanted to bury myself inside of. I know you don't want to pretend to be my girlfriend, but it could benefit us both in so many ways."

I jerk back, nearly tipping over in my seat. "Jesus Christ, Roland. Didn't I tell you never to talk around me that way again?" My eyes flick to Liam, whose gaze narrows on me in question. I can see the concern in his expression, but I ignore it and turn my gaze back to Roland.

"Shit." He rubs his palm down his face. "I'm sorry, Izzy. Look—I didn't sleep much. I rarely do. But I drank a bit more than I intended, and coupled with the nightmares I still have occasionally, well. It was one of those nights."

"Nightmares?" I cross my arms over my chest, which, of course, causes his eyes to flicker to my breasts. "You still have nightmares?

I thought you stopped having those back in high school." I remember a time when he would come to school looking worse for wear—he never told me about them, just that he dealt with them. It made sense seeing as he witnessed his mother being pushed to her death by his father. But I'm surprised to hear he is still dealing with them.

"Never mind. I shouldn't have said anything about it. All that matters is I'm running on like four hours of sleep. So don't be a bitch."

I reel back from him, startled by his callous response. I open my mouth to scold him for being an asshole, but he blows out a breath and closes his eyes, groaning. "Just tell me the plan, Freckles."

The nickname he gave me in school creates a feeling I don't want to acknowledge, so I push them aside for now. I've done nothing but think about his *other* problems all night. Barely sleeping a wink between our encounter and my mixed-up emotions, I came up with a solution he's going to hate. And after hearing his confession about having nightmares still, I know it's the right one. I *hate* seeing him like this—the Roland I remember was fun and filled with so much love. Seeing *this* version, I can't decide which was a lie and if this one is the phony.

With his hand still clutched in mine, I brush my thumb over his knuckles. "I think you need to take some time off after your last show in a few weeks. Tell the label you're burnt out and need to rest and, while you're doing that, get some *help*. I think you have a serious problem with relationships, Roland. I don't know what your parent's marriage was like before—well, you know. But I can imagine it wasn't the greatest example of 'healthy' seeing how it ended. It's done something to you, tainting your view on sex and possibly love and, if I'm right—the reason for your destructive behavior."

Roland makes a clicking sound with his tongue. "You think I need some head doctor?"

"Liam, can you give us a minute?" I tilt my head at the monster of a man watching us with deep concern. The lines etched in his brow tell me he's just as worried about Roland as I am.

He glances between Roland and me. "You sure you two are alright?"

"Yes. We're fine."

I'm not sure how *that* nonchalant remark from Roland convinces him to leave us, but I watch in shock as he exits the room.

"I do, Roland. You need to talk to *someone*." I hold his gaze. "And since you don't ever want to elaborate on the nightmares you say you're still occasionally having... I'll bet they have something to do with your past. A past that's made you into this man. You think I'm stupid, Roland, but I know what you went through when you were a kid. And *anyone* who witnessed that kind of trauma needs to talk to someone. You can't work through it alone."

"You *think* you know me? You don't know shit. And I did talk with someone, Isabella, *remember*? A lot of 'someones' if we're being honest. My aunt made sure I had the best therapists around. And yet—I still turned out to be this fucked up guy you can't stand."

Standing up, I pace beside him. "Can't stand you? Jesus Christ, Roland, this isn't a dig at you. But... I'm worried about you." As I say the words, I realize how much I mean them. Somehow, in the last few months, this idiot of a man has worked his way under my skin again. And that's dangerous for my heart. "And after what happened between us... you're losing whatever control you may have had and you're spiraling... what if you do something that results in someone pressing charges?"

"That's laughable. The women I *do* fuck… are all consenting, Izzy. They like to dominate me—it's not the other way around. Don't you get it? That's the man I am. I crave the dominance someone gives me because it keeps me in line."

Yeah… I figured he'd say that—it's his crutch. The jacked-up wall he's erected around his heart and soul to make himself feel better. But the truth is, I know that's not him. He might say I don't know him, but I do. He's the fucking guy I've compared every man I've dated to, because he was—no, *is* that good of a guy. I just need to piece his life back together and stop the bleeding mess he's making of his career to show him that.

Looking at the shell of a man sitting here, my heart stutters inside my chest. Roland was the boy I thought I'd marry… but like most teenage love, it fizzled out and died when greener pastures started calling. But his memory never did. I loved him fiercely and losing him hurt like a bitch. And despite the way things have been going, my body still burns for his touch. Only, I won't be telling *him* that —exactly.

Turning to Roland, I give him a halfhearted smile. "I don't want our past to interfere with what I'm trying to do, Roland. And while allowing what we did to happen was a complete fuck up on my part, it wasn't entirely unwanted. The thing is, I don't want to see you lose yourself and push boundaries with someone else. Someone who could cause you issues, especially of the legal variety."

The bright blue eyes snap up and pin me with a fiery gaze. "Excuse me? What do you mean, it wasn't unwanted?"

Waving my hand in the air. "Don't focus on the first part, Roland. Focus on the *'someone who could cause you issues'* part of the comment. You could do something that lands you in jail and not even your brother could get you out. You've got to get your needs under control and stop letting your dick lead you into trouble. From where I'm standing, you wouldn't know control if it bit you in the ass."

Roland stands on his feet, and with his eyes locked on mine, inches toward me. "No. I think I want to know what you mean." He crowds toward me, backing me against the wall. "What does *not entirely unwanted* mean, Freckles?"

"Roland." I brace my hand against his chest, halting his forward movement. "Stop calling me that and back up."

"What. Did. You. Mean?"

His body is practically vibrating with a charged current of lust. "Roland, you're insanely hot. You don't need me to tell you to know that. I'm also not going to stand here and lie to you. This isn't meant to stroke your ego, but I might still have a slight crush on you. But... after what happened, I just —." His lips crash into mine and all words die on my tongue. A tongue he's currently sucking into his mouth. This kiss is unlike anything we've shared before. It's demanding. It's hot. It's fucking *ruining* me for any other man. The feel of his keen hard-on pressing against me brings me back to reality and I break free.

"No. We can't do this, Roland. I told you it's too dangerous for us to go there. Plus, I won't be part of the problem. You get away with whatever you want without consequence. Shit... you can have whoever you want. I'm already a notch on your conquest belt—let's leave any semblance of *us* in the past. I'm a woman who doesn't do casual, and you *only* do casual. I hate myself for wanting you, but with what happened in my apartment, I know I can't be just a *play-thing* to you. We've got too much history and I have very little of my heart left to risk it."

"Izzy." He steps into me, but I press him back.

"No, Roland.' I close my eyes. "The man I give what's left of my heart will have to put me first. I won't be his toy, nor will I compromise who I am. That's not something you can commit to—and you've already made me hate myself for wanting the impossible. Please... just let me do my job and go on my way. Like we *agreed*. I fix your career and life and you get the hell out of mine."

"What if—" Roland is cut off when someone comes into the room.

"Sorry to interrupt." Harold strolls in the room, his eyes curious about our current state. "Everything alright here?"

"Sure is." Roland moves toward the couch and sits down. "We were just discussing her new plan, since she won't be my girlfriend."

"*Pretend* Girlfriend."

"Right. *Pretend* Girlfriend." My hands ball into fists at my sides. I want to strangle him, but that's a turn on for him, not punishment. Roland notices the movement and catches my gaze. Jesus Christ, he smirks like he knows exactly what I'm thinking. Unfurling my hands, I flex my fingers instead of throat punching him in front of Harold and giving him what he thinks he wants.

Harold glances between us again, his expression curious. "Ok then. Well, Miss Holiday. How are you going to fix this mess?"

I swear to God the look Roland still has on his face makes me want to say fuck it and punch him square in the throat, but instead I clear my throat and force out a fake smile. "To fix *his* mess, Roland needs to take a hiatus after his last show. He needs to seek some counseling for his reckless behavior and other *issues* he has going on - like his inability to take responsibility for anything he does. We can tell the public he is taking a break to focus on music, but the truth will be he's getting himself straight. Otherwise, the next fuckup will be something he lands in jail for."

"And Roland? How do you feel about this suggestion?"

The fucking death glare Roland gives me makes the hair on my neck stand up and I know I'm not going to like whatever cockamamie response he has. "I'm fine with the suggestion. But I have one condition that I expect to happen if you want me to agree."

Harold cocks an eyebrow at him. "You're not really in a place to make demands, but I'll hear it."

With the smuggest expression I've ever seen on him, Roland cocks an eyebrow and spits out the biggest bullshit request ever. "I want Miss Holiday to live with me and shadow me twenty-four seven. Like a babysitter of sorts."

"Absolutely Not."

"I love it." Harold speaks at the same time as me, his smile telling me Roland's ridiculous demand will be unavoidable.

*Check. Fucking. Mate.*

"Great. Miss Holiday and I will head out now to move all her belongings into my penthouse. Send over any paperwork you need her and I to sign. Otherwise, I'll see *you* at this weekend's show."

Harold leaves me staring into the eyes of Roland Winston as he smirks with a knowing grin. I stand, my fingers tightly wound into a fist, desperately trying *not* to follow through on my thoughts to strike him. "This is complete bullshit, and you know it."

He smiles as he pushes his hands into his pockets. "Bullshit or not, let's go get your shit... *roomie.*"

Roland turns around and heads out of the room. I have no choice but to follow him. His long legs make it challenging for me to catch up, but as soon as we reach the parking lot outside, I finally do, and grab hold of his arm. "Call Harold and tell him this is a dumb idea.

I'm not moving in with you. Hell, I planned to *quit* less than twenty-four hours ago."

Roland spins me around and slams me against his car. "You mean after I kissed you—right? You planned on quitting because of what happened between us." His eyes fill with remorse for the first time since arriving at the studio.

Shrugging my shoulder, I nod. "Yes, and no. Roland, what *we* did was…" My words are cut off as his lips press into mine. As much as he sends a blaze of fire through my veins, I can't let him do this again. Not now—maybe not *ever*. Pressing my palms flat against his chest, I shove him back. *"Don't."*

Shoving him a little harder a second time, I manage to put enough space between us to climb under his arm and slip around him.

"Wait." Roland snatches my arm. "Look… can we start over?"

"Rich coming from a man who basically ordered me to live in his house. How about I just go get my things and meet you at your place? We can figure out the rest later."

Roland opens his mouth to respond, but his phone interrupts. Holding his finger up to silence me, he presses the device to his ear. "What? Yeah… are you serious? Fine." I watch as he pockets the device. "I'll meet you there."

Leaving me rooted to the spot, I watch as Roland climbs into his car and pulls forward out of the spot. I have no idea what the phone call was about, but based on his shitty attitude, I can only assume it wasn't pleasant. I can already tell living with him is going to be an absolute nightmare. Not to mention this fucked-up attraction I have for him.

Snapping from my shocked state, I climb into my own car. I'd had enough forethought to drive myself here, which I'm grateful for now. I need to think, and driving will afford me the time. As I start my car's engine, I let out the breath I've been unconsciously hold-ing. Navigating my way out onto the streets, I realize I need to loop in my boss on the hot mess express that is now my job—and life, apparently.

The sound of the phone ringing echoes through my car's interior. His voice creates a multitude of tension as it fills the tiny space.

"Izzy—how's it going?"

Signaling to pull out, I keep my eyes on the road as I begin to fill him in. A few simple grunts and uh-huhs are all I get out of him. He takes their side on the matter, encouraging me that this is good for my career and might be the key to saving his. Of course, he doesn't know what's brewing between Roland and me—and I don't plan on telling him… or anyone.

My nerves are frayed as I pull into my spot at the apartment build-ing. Apparently, Roland owns another just like it in our hometown of Atlanta. When he's not touring, he splits his time between here and there, which means we'll be back on our home turf soon. Staring at the monstrosity in front of me, I wonder what it's like to be him. He's had more money than God since he was a kid and being a top ten musician, only added zeroes to his bank account. Climbing out, I scan the lot. I wouldn't be surprised if Roland is already in his apartment waiting for me. Each step I take feels like a lamb walking to their slaughter.

When I enter the lobby, Sam, the building's guard, greets me. "Miss Holiday, Mr. Winston instructed me to have your things moved into his penthouse. There are several guys waiting outside your apart-ment now."

Grunting my displeasure, I forced a smile at him, anyway. "I'm surprised he didn't just have you move it without me."

"Oh, he tried. But I'm not about to have a woman pissed because I went through her things. My wife would cut off my balls."

Unable to hide my laugh, I grin for the first time all morning. "I appreciate that—but it's not your balls getting cut off today. Thank you, Sam. I guess I'll head on up. I'm sure His *Majesty* is waiting."

# 5

# Roland

BEING STUCK IN THIS LARGE, yet cramped hotel is making me lose my mind. It's been a month since Izzy begrudgingly moved in with me—and she hasn't made it pleasant. After leaving Nashville, we came to Chicago. And I swear if I'm not plotting ways to kill her, I'm trying to figure out how to get in her pants.

Everything about her makes me crazy with need, which is exactly why I'm going out tonight. "I'll be back." I shoot her a glance as I head toward the front door. "I need to blow off some steam and being here isn't helping."

"Where are you going?" She lifts her head from the couch, pinning me with a knowing look. "You know you can't just go hang out at a bar."

"I'm not. Don't *worry* about it, Freckles."

Slamming the door before she can nag me any longer, I find myself inside the elevator. Visiting the local club here is the last thing I *should* do, but exactly what I *need*, so I tell the driver to take me to Club Erotica. As soon as the car stops out front, I slide out and tell him to come back in two hours. That's more than enough time to let some of my demons out to play. Tonight, I need to let someone else take control to break me down.

Stepping inside, I'm met with the dark, classy interior of the main lobby. After checking in, I make my way to the bar, eager to find a Top who can give me the punishment I need. After the incident with Izzy, I've been feeling overwhelmed with guilt because she's right. I let my attraction blind me and nearly put myself in a position even my brother couldn't get me out of.

"Hey there, sexy." The smooth voice washes over me like fine silk. "Haven't seen you here before."

The woman brushes her palm down my shirt, gripping the collar as she tugs me toward her body. "I'm just visiting… for work." I shrug my shoulders as the thrill of her touch sends tiny electric currents across my skin. "You free tonight?" Glancing around the club, I don't see anyone who appears to be with her.

"You need some discipline tonight, baby boy? Because I'm a Domme—not a submissive."

Dropping my eyes to the ground, I murmur as my balls tingle with anticipation. "Yes, Mistress."

"Follow me."

Striding behind her, I keep my eyes trained on the back of her boots. I know how this works—it's what I crave. To be controlled and ruled over makes my body feel alive. My therapist says it has to do with the lack of real parental guidance growing up, coupled with the abuse I saw. I seek out someone who can stifle the anger building inside me.

The clicking of the door jolts me from my thoughts, and I realize we've already arrived at the private playroom. Silently, I wait for the instructions I know are coming.

"Tell me baby boy. Why do you need this tonight?"

Fighting the war inside me for even being here, I mutter my response. "I fucked up, Mistress."

She reaches out, her long crimson nails tracing along my chest, coming to rest beneath my chin. Mistress tilts my chin up. "Tell me."

"I let my demons control me and I tried to take something I wasn't supposed to—and I still want it, even though it can't be mine."

She tilts her head as if to inspect me more thoroughly. "I see. A woman?"

Sighing, I squeeze my eyes shut and nod. "Yes."

"And this woman…" She brushes her hand down my chest, her palm cupping my groin as she settles it between my legs. "Who is she to you?"

"An old friend—and we crossed a boundary we shouldn't have. She's not dealing with it well and keeps pushing me away." The pain in my chest intensifies and I mumble. "Everyone pushes me away."

"And you feel like you've done something wrong? Something that warrants being punished?" Her fingers dig into my sac, squeezing my balls in her fist. The pressure makes me grunt, but I welcome the pain.

"Yes, Mistress."

She lets go, stepping away from my body. "Strip and kneel, baby boy. Tonight's going to push you to the limits. What's your safe word?"

"Red, Mistress."

She pats my ass. "Do you have any hard boundaries when it comes to a scene?"

"Condoms have to be used." I strip the clothing from my body. Stepping to the center of the room, I drop to a kneeling position and wait. Time feels like it's moving at a snail's pace as I listen to the sounds of her moving around the suite. I have no idea what *her* idea of punishment entails, but whatever she chooses, I've earned. My mind drifts to Izzy, creating a sharp pain inside my chest.

"Stand and face me."

I do as she instructs, completely nude, and watch as she grabs hold of my cock. The smooth metal that clamps around it tells me exactly what I'm in store for. The click of the lock and the weight of the contraption causes me to inhale sharply. She tugs my hand into hers, guiding me over the corner where a Tachigaeru Bondage Chair is nestled. Pushing me down, she clamps my wrists into the restraints, doing the same with my feet, spreading me wide open. This chair makes me completely vulnerable to whatever she wants to do to me. I watch as she circles the chair with a devilish grin on her face.

"You've been a bad boy, baby boy. It's time to test your boundaries." She slides the hood she's holding over my head, cutting off my vision. "Remember to use your safe word if needed."

Knowing my pain threshold is a bit higher than previously antici-pated, Mistress places clamps on my nipples and tugs at the chain connecting them. Slight discomfort—like pinching sensations — creates a flurry of goosebumps on my skin. The rush of blood to my head heightens the sensitivity painfully growing between my legs as Mistress applies more pressure with her clamps. I grunt and strain against the restraints holding me in place, the need for release building from her torturous pleasure. Shifting my thighs together to stave off some of the pressure in my balls, Mistress slaps my leg.

"Don't get any ideas." Her voice sounds muffled behind the black hood covering my head. "I'm in control and this is your punishment, baby boy. You won't get to cum—not unless I say so."

I can hear her footsteps behind me, but I'm completely unprepared for the feel of something hard and cool being pressed into my ass. I grunt at the intrusion, my body clenching out of instinct as a wave of pleasure ripples through me. She presses harder as she slides an arm across my neck from behind and pulls back, cutting off some of my air flow as she holds me in place.

"You're a good boy," she whispers against my neck. "Take it all."

Once it's settled firmly between my cheeks, she lets go of my body and steps away. I don't know how I'm not in more pain. The cage sitting firmly around my dick is painfully constricting, staunching the flow of blood. A part of me wants to beg her to take it off, but I don't. I deserve this and more.

The sensation of her fingers grazing my hard shaft makes me jump. I'm hypersensitive from the cock cage and the slight touch of her nail sends my body into overload. I can't stop the moaning that slips free. "Oh, *fuck.*" My hips buck involuntarily, and she growls at my disobedience. The sound threatens to cause my dick to combust inside the metal contraption.

She bites my inner thigh, making me shudder with need. Her soft lips suck on the sensitive skin, causing me to squirm uncontrollably in response. My hands are trapped above me, but it doesn't matter —I know when she finally sets me free from the confines of the dick prison, I'll cum like the fourth of July.

Even in my heightened state, my mind wanders to a fiery redhead consuming my every breath lately. The way her body flushed at my touch, not to mention the little whimpers she tried to stifle but couldn't no matter how hard she fought it, makes my cock turn to steel just thinking about it. Despite her not pushing me away, a smidge of regret consumes me for treating her like a whore. And that guilt has led me here, bound, and hooded, seeking punishment.

Izzy's not here with me now, though. Instead, I'm with a woman who is more than willing to help me get off. It's a good thing, too, because I need it badly. My balls ache for release, and my cock is so hard it hurts. But there's only one woman I want—and she's barely speaking to me.

"You're doing so well, Baby Boy." Mistress says in a sultry voice. "But I want to play—ok? Can I let your cock out for some fun?" She steps closer and runs her hands down my chest until they reach the cage.

"Yes, Mistress. Protection first." I never have sex without a condom and since this is my first time doing a scene with her, I remind her of my boundaries. I can't risk an unplanned pregnancy with anyone —I'll never be father material.

Mistress removes the metal barrier. The contraption snaps open and falls away to the floor. My cock springs up as it is freed of its prison, throbbing eagerly for attention. The pins and needle sensation skittering up my spine makes me whimper in desperation. Knowing what I need, she takes my hardening member into her mouth. Her tongue swirls around my head before she engulfs me completely, causing me to buck into her throat. She moans with each deep swallow that pulls me deeper down her gullet.

"Oh, *fuck!*" I cry out, thrusting my hips forward into her hot mouth. She humps my shaft between her lips, bobbing her head back and forth. Just when I think I'm going to explode in her throat, she pulls off, leaving my body burning in the seat.

"Don't cum, Baby Boy. Not yet."

Willing my body not to spill my seed, I take several deep breaths beneath the darkness of the hood, shielding my eyes. The tug of the chain against my chest makes me startle, but when I feel her rolling a condom down my engorged length, I blow out a breath.

"You've been a bad boy. But Mistress wants to cum. Can Mistress cum on your cock?"

Not recognizing my own voice, I rasp out, "Yes, Mistress."

"Good… I've enlisted some help to make this more interesting. What's your safe word?"

"Red." My hackles rise, not knowing what's coming. "Mistress?"

"Silence, Baby Boy. I won't do anything to hurt you—more than I already have."

A pair of rough hands grip my hips from behind. The intense pressure of the metal plug between my cheeks being jerked from my body without warning causes me to hiss as a wave of pleasurable pain radiates from my now-empty ass. I tense as the fingers probe my hole, pressing inside and moving around inside me. I've had plenty of anal plugs shoved in there, but another person's fingers? Never.

The feel of Mistress straddling my thighs is the only warning I get before she impales herself over my shaft. Her locks brush against my chest, confirming she's sitting on me reverse cowboy. My ass clenches when I feel the moist tip of a tongue dipping into my backside.

"Fuck." I grunt at the intrusion. And despite the uncertainty of what's happening, I can't deny the pleasure that suddenly ripples through me.

"Boy—I didn't tell you to *lick* him. Come around here." My mind stutters with the Boy name she uses—a man just had his tongue inside my ass.

"Mistress." I growl out her name. "I didn't agree with *that*."

"You can use your safe word. Otherwise, shut up. He's here to fuck me. I needed two cocks tonight, Baby boy—even *if* yours is exceptional."

I feel her rise off me, and the same callous hand circles my shaft. "Guide him into my asshole, boy."

My tip is poised at her opening as he guides her down. The pressure of her muscles clamping down around my shaft nearly undoes me, but the sudden removal of the nipple clamps still my thoughts. The tingling feeling sends jolts of pleasure straight to my sac, and I have to close my eyes and count backwards in my head to avoid cumming until she tells me I can.

Her body leans into me, her back pressed against my front. I hear her command the man in the room to shove his steel rod into her awaiting cunt. The force of his thrust rocks her into me, shifting her against my cock. I shift my hips up, thrusting into her from below, my body moving on its own.

Her pants and moans drive me to near insanity when I finally hear the words I've needed for the last thirty minutes.

"I'm going to cum... Baby Boy—fill my ass up as I clamp down on the boy's dick."

Even as my body spurts with the force of my release, the only thing filling my vision is the one person I came here to forget. Even with the punishment... the torment that's consumed me for years is nothing compared to the pain I feel when I shout *her* name into the room, giving into the orgasm as it rips from my spine, and I spill into the condom.

"*Izzy.*"

# 6

# Izzy

THE LAST THING I expected was to find Roland stumbling into the apartment at three am—but that's exactly what's happening.

"What the fuck, Roland? Where the hell have you been? We leave for New York in less than three hours."

Roland brushes past me, ignoring my words. "Leave me alone, Izzy. I'm going to bed."

Rage like nothing I've felt bubbles up and I explode. I've worked my ass off to keep his goddamn name out of the media and what does he do—goes out and does God knows what to land himself splashed all over the front page of every media outlet.

"No... I won't. We've done a lot to clean your image up, Roland. I need to know if there's a possibility from whatever you've been doing to come back and bite us in the ass."

He snorts as he tugs a glass out of the cabinet and grabs a bottle of vodka from the mini-fridge. "Don't worry. No one knew who I was, and nobody filmed me this time."

"Jesus Christ." I run my fingers through my messy locks. "You don't know that Roland. You have no idea what someone is capable of."

He slams the glass down. The clank echoing through the room. "You are absolutely right. I have no idea what anyone is capable of—Lord knows I wouldn't have thought my own father would kill my mother after spending years raping her in front of me. Or that my brother... the man I look up to, could shoot the bastard. But *that's* exactly what happened. Excuse me for not knowing or exactly giving a fuck what runs through people's minds."

I gasp at the admission he's finally shared. It's what I've been wanting to hear from him since falling back into his life, but not like this. And I'm pretty sure it's the first time he's admitted this out loud. "Your father was a monster, Roland."

"And he *sired* me—his spawn."

Jesus... he's convinced himself he's just as evil as the man who made him. Taking several timid steps toward him, I stop right in front of him. "You're not him, Roland."

"Yep, you're right—I'm my mother, Izzy. She took his beatings, and I'm just like her." He presses his palms to the countertop. "Yet *I* seek them out because the only love I ever knew from the bastard was pain. You don't get it. You can't. You're too kind—too... pure."

"Pure?" I laugh. "No, Roland. I'm not. I've made mistakes, making me far from pure. And kind? I've been called a bitch plenty in my career. It's for show, though. Just like this image you've created for yourself. You've convinced yourself you need these things, but I think you're wrong."

His head bobs not as he speaks. "I wish that were true, but I *crave* the violence—dominance. I *need* it, Izzy. Again... you'd never understand. It's just one more way I'm irreversibly broken. Just leave me alone. I'm damaged and you can't *fix* me."

He turns to walk away, but I'm too fucking pissed to let him go. Storming after him, I grab his arm and dig into his flesh with my nails. "Stop." I jerk him back, halting his footsteps.

Using my body weight, I push him against the wall and lean into him, caging him against it as best I can as I lower my voice to a near-growl. "You need what, Roland? *This?*" I thread my fingers through his hair and pull the blonde strands hard. His eyes widen in shock as I cup his balls and squeeze. "So, what... you like it a little kinky. There's nothing wrong with being creative with sex, Roland. But *where* you do that matters."

I yank on his hair again, pulling his face down to meet my lips. He goes willingly, allowing me to control the kiss - one that's setting me on fire, too. He groans as I bite down on his lip and my hand slips beneath his shirt. Needing the material off, I let go of his head and fist the material in my hands. Giving it a hard jerk, I send the button flying across the floor. The tiny plastic disk skitters against the laminate floor, clattering way louder than I expected. I wedge my knee between his legs and scrape my nails down his chest, tracing the massive tattoo covering his muscles. The ink only adds to the beauty of his skin, highlighting the definition of his body.

Roland hisses, "Izzy—what are you doing?"

Covering his mouth with my hand, I snap at him. "Shut up, Roland. You're not allowed to talk." I fumble with his belt, finally getting it free and allowing me to unbutton his trousers. Shoving my hand inside, I find him hard as steel, the tip dripping with pre-cum and begging for attention. "You like this, don't you?" I wrap my fingers around his shaft and squeeze. Roland opens his mouth to talk, but I shut him up by wrapping my fingers around his throat. My hands are tiny compared to his broad neck, so they barely cover the span of his meaty flesh. But it doesn't matter, the move has his dick jumping in my grasp.

"Izzy." He moans my name, closing his eyes as his head leans back against the wall.

My body is flooding with desire, so I let go of his neck and jerk my hand from his cock. Stepping back, I hold his gaze as I tug the t-shirt I'd been sleeping in over my head and toss it to the floor. Standing in front of him completely naked, I know I'm about to cross a line I can't take back—but I don't care. I'm too far gone now.

Pulling his hair, I slam my lips over his and shove my tongue inside. When he meets mine with just as much desire, I bite down. The tang of blood hits my senses, but instead of feeling disgust, my pussy clenches. Grabbing his hand, which is still balled in a fist against his leg, I drag it between my legs.

"Touch me." I mumble against his mouth, but he keeps his fingers closed. "Fucking, touch me, Rols." I can feel the tension in his body, like he's uncertain how to proceed. Using my free hand, I pinch his nipple and twist mercilessly. "Fingers, Roland. Put them inside me. Right. *Now.*"

Like a trigger, he explodes into action. His fingers unfurl and slip between my folds. He hisses against my lips, his tongue dueling with mine as he plunges in and out of my channel.

My body tightens with pleasure, and I know it's not going to take much to send me soaring. "Make me cum, Roland."

He breaks the kiss, trailing his lips down my neck and latches onto my throat. His other arm finally moves as he uses it to half lift one leg off the floor. He rams his hand between my thighs, his digits moving at a relentless pace. It feels filthy, but I need more.

"Take out your dick, Rols. I need you to fuck me." I push his pants down, urging him to comply. When his cock springs free, I grip it in my palm and give it a tug. He groans against my flesh, pulling his fingers from my slick cunt and using his hand to lift me completely off the floor.

Before I can ask what he's doing, Roland reverses our positions and slams me against the wall, plunging his shaft deep inside me. His cock stretches me to the hilt, and I toss my head back, resting it on the sheetrock helping hold me up. Tugging his hair like a bridle, I ride him as hard as my body will allow. His thrusts threaten to split me in two, but it's pushing me toward a release that I'm certain I'll regret later.

"Fuck, Freckles." He pounds into me, his shaft stroking deep inside me.

The tingles start in my feet, traveling at light speed through my veins and pooling in my belly. "Roland." I cry out, my walls clamping down on his dick like they're holding him in a vice grip. If his cock was responsible for providing him oxygen, I have no doubt my pussy just cut off his air supply. He cries out, unable to fight the war raging inside him, and his hot cum fills me. Our ragged breaths fill the hallway of the suite as he pulls out and drops my legs to the ground.

Roland blinks, like he's seeing me for the first time tonight, and takes a step back. "Fuck." I watch as he takes a step back, shaking his head like he's alarmed. "I shouldn't have done that."

"Shouldn't have done *what*? Roland, *I* did this. I *wanted* this. You need to see you're not a monster. What we just did was fucking hot."

He swipes his hand down his face as I cover my breasts with my arms. He grabs the pants pooling at his feet and tugs them up his hips. His flaccid cock drips from our coupling as he shoves himself into his pants, his head bobbing back and forth on his neck.

"This proves I'm a monster, Izzy. What you did turned me on so fucking much I couldn't breathe until I was buried inside you. And I fucked you after—" his words die and I suck in a breath, seeing the sheen of tears in his eyes.

"After you what, Roland?"

"You deserve better, Izzy. Not a man who's so fucking destroyed from his childhood that he needs to be manhandled by a woman to get off. I can't love like you deserve. And God, you deserve that, Freckles. You're light and I'm darkness. I'm sorry for tonight. I'm sorry I let my black heart cloud your sun."

I watch as he turns and practically runs from me. I hurry behind him, but I'm met with the door as he slams himself inside his room. The click of the lock is like a slap to the face, and I slam my hands against the door—not caring about the fact I'm naked as the day I was born.

"Roland... don't do this. Please. You're not the fucking darkness— and even if you are, the dark still needs the light." When I hear the sound of his sob echo from behind the wooden barrier, I press my head against the door. "I'm sorry, Rols... I'm sorry I couldn't save you back then."

I walk away from his door, my own tears streaming down my face. Grabbing my discarded shirt off the ground, I wipe the sticky mess from between my legs and stumble into my room. Throwing myself into my bed, I curl onto my side and let the tears free flow. I can't fix him—he's going to have to want to do that for himself. But what I *can* do is fix his career... and no matter what happens now, that's exactly what I'll do. Roland deserves to be happy—even if it means my heart shatters into a million pieces.

Because as the hot tears fall onto my pillow, I realize something... I never stopped loving him and what little I had left of my heart is going to crumble, anyway.

# 7

# Izzy

FOUR WEEKS of pure torture and we're finally back in Atlanta for the show. Too bad my anger has reached epic proportions. Roland hasn't spoken to me since we slept together in Chicago. *Snort.* Sleeping together is far from what we did—hell, I can *still* feel him between my legs. The concert in New York and then Virginia felt like a prison sentence with the way he's avoided me like the plague. After tonight, we leave for New Orleans and then Phoenix. Austin is the last stop—so he'll have no choice but to face me before then. We *need* to talk because the icy environment we're living in can't go on.

"Where's Roland?" I glance over at the sound manager, who simply shrugs.

"No clue. I know his brothers are due to watch the show—maybe he went to meet them."

Grumbling under my breath, I huff out a frustrated breath. "Thanks."

Stepping up to the closed door of Roland's private dressing room, I raise my hand to knock, but pause. The sound of a deep voice filters through the wooden barrier.

"I've missed you, little brother." The muffled sound of slapping tells me whoever it is had just hugged Roland. Or maybe knocked some sense into him, but I wouldn't be that lucky. "How the hell have you been?"

"Good. The tour is almost done, so I'll be home in a few months. I'm ready for a break."

"A break?"

"Is something wrong?" The deep voice sounds concerned at his admission. Honestly, so am I and despite my inner voice telling me not to, I press my ear against the door. "You've *never* taken a break."

I hear who I assume is Roland blowing out a breath. "I know. But I'm exhausted. I want to slow down and maybe write some new music. I've been moving non-stop for the last eighteen months and just need—"

"Rest. I get it. You deserve to stop and enjoy the fruits of your hard work, Rol. No need to explain."

Not wanting to feel like I'm spying, I push open the door and pause like I wasn't just eavesdropping. "Mr. Winston." Three sets of eyes land on me. "They're asking for you backstage."

"Right." Roland stands and pops his neck. "Tell them I'll be right up, Isabella."

I turn and leave quickly before his brothers recognize me. The fact he called me Isabella tells me more than I'm ready to accept. I slow when I hear my name through the open door.

"Isabella?"

"She's my—public relations manager. The label seemed to think I needed help with my image. They hired her six months ago."

"Your image? What the fuck does that mean?" Drake, his brother, growls in question.

"Apparently being caught in photos with various women is sending my fans the wrong message. Whatever. She just keeps the media at bay. No big deal."

"If you say so, little brother. But from the sound out there. Your fans seem to love you just the same."

"I gotta go. If she comes back here, she'll bust my balls for sure."

I hurry down the hallway, fighting the mental image that Roland's words deposit in my mind, and make my way to the spot behind the stage where I can watch him perform. He doesn't know I do this every show, but seeing him in his element reminds me, beneath all that bullshit persona he's built for himself—he is passionate about *something*.

His brothers take a perch near the entrance to the stage. And though I can't hear exactly what the one he called Gage says, I get the gist. They think I'm here because of a few pictures taken with a supermodel. It makes me wonder if they know the true depths of his sexual depravity. Maybe they're just like him—maybe the whole family is fucked up. I read and heard enough about them through the gossip, to know their father was a psycho and killed their mother, but Roland's confession in Chicago cemented this. He never wanted to talk about his parents in school, but I knew it was bad—*hell,* everyone knew what happened. It made local news, and most hadn't forgotten about it by the time he and I were in high school. I only know about his brothers, though, because before tonight, I had never actually met them. Both were off in college when he and I dated. But seeing them here now, there's no denying the Winston brothers hit the gene pool lottery. Turning back to the stage, I focus on Roland, and my heart skips a beat.

The first chords of his music send chills down my arms. It's a new song he just released and a part of me wonders if it's a silent plea for something more. I close my eyes and let the words wash over me.

*Can't you see me*

*Can't you hear*

*My heart is screaming*

*My mind is breaking*


*You think you know me*

*You think it's love*

*This feeling is burning*

*Deep inside my body*


*You need someone worthy*

*You need someone good*

*Your soul is on fire*

*Burning up in flames*


*Can't you see the darkness*

*It's coming for you*

*That moment of desperation*

*When we both fall*


*Cut your losses*

*Run far away*

*Before there's no turning back*

*And your heart can't be saved*


*I was the poison*

*That polluted your blood.*

*I was the wrecking ball*

*That destroyed it all.*


*Can't you see me*

*Can't you hear*

*My heart is screaming*

*My mind is breaking*


*Can't you see me*

*Can't you hear*

*My heart is screaming*

*My mind is breaking*


*Please see me*

*Please save me*

*Make this pain all disappear*

*Make this pain all disappear*

I know Roland is close to taking an intermission for a water and cool off break, and as much as I hate to interrupt his reunion with his brothers, I can't wait any longer. I need to know how we're supposed to keep going like this. Moving closer to his brothers, I take up a perch at the edge of the side entrance and wait. I know I pushed him, and maybe I shouldn't have, but he needed to see someone capable of accepting him and his desires. Even though my eyes are watching the man on stage, I overhear his brother's conversation just behind me.

"Fuck." His brother Gage presses the cellphone to his ear. "This is Dr. Winston."

I peer over my shoulder as I watch the handsome, older man's expression turn grim as he fusses into his phone. "Hastings, I'm not on call tonight. Call Peterson." His frustration is evident as he pinches the bridge of his nose. Grunting in disgust, he growls. "Fine. I'll be there as soon as I can." Shoving the phone in his pocket, Gage turns toward his brother.

"Everything alright?" Drake says, his eyes narrowing with concern.

"No. I have to go." He glances back at Roland on stage, then back at Drake.

"What? *Now?*"

"Apparently there's a judge in the waiting room demanding I come and see his wife. It sounds bad and the hospital board has requested my presence." The guilt of having to cut the visit short shows like a neon sign in the dark.

"Let's tell Roland we're leaving."

"You can stay. I'll just grab an Uber." Gage gives Drake a dark look that screams authority, but the younger man isn't having it.

"Not a chance. If a judge is expecting you to drop your life and come in, I'm going with you. I want to make sure there isn't any unscrupulous intent behind this demand."

At that same moment, Roland wraps up his song and tells the crowd that nature calls, and he needs to take care of business—which makes the stadium erupt into laughter.

"Whatdidya think?" Roland pops the lid to a water bottle and chugs its contents.

"Fantastic, as usual. Look." His brother grips his shoulder. "I have to go. The hospital board called and demanded I come for a VIP patient."

"Really? Who is it? The King of Persia?" Roland chuckles.

"No, a local judge. And he's making a scene in the ER."

"You're going with him, right?" Roland turns toward Drake as I stand off to the side, watching their interaction like some kind of voyeur.

"Of course. This request reeks of desperation and unscrupulousness." He nods, his words relaxing Roland slightly.

"Good. Call me when you're done. Maybe you can meet up with me for a drink. I don't leave until tomorrow. Last stop is Austin, then home for a few months."

"Will do, little bro. Good show. I don't think your fans have lost their liking for you yet." Drake pats his back.

Not wanting to waste another moment, I interrupt their goodbyes. "Roland."

"Isabella." Roland's voice takes on a weird tone, making his brother shoot him a confused look. "These are my brothers, Gage and Drake." He motions to them.

"Um, we kinda met earlier, remember? But hi. I go by Izzy, *please*. Roland talks a lot about you." I cut my eyes back to him. "Can we talk for a moment?"

Roland stiffens, and I watch as the blood drains from his face. "*Now?*" His voice is laden with aggravation.

"Please?" I place my hand on his arm, only to have him jerk away like my touch burns. Gage glances between us. "You good?"

"Yeah. Let me know how it goes." I can feel his brother's eyes on us as he turns and slowly follows me toward his dressing room.

"What the *fuck*, Isabella? This couldn't wait? You had to interrupt what little time I get with my brothers?"

I close my eyes and take a deep breath before turning to face him. "You're shutting me out and I can't do my job."

He grunts as he shoves his hands into the pockets of his frayed jeans. "Your job—I see. This is about your *job*." Roland sucks his teeth in irritation. "And me keeping my distance is making it hard for you? I'm shutting you out?"

Narrowing my eyes on him, I snap. "You know what I'm talking about."

"No." He steps forward, backing me into the wall. "I don't think I do, *Isabella*."

"Roland." I press my hand against his chest, my breath hitching at the feel of his hard muscles beneath my touch. He's like a drug tugging on my sanity, trying to make me relapse.

He wedges his knee between my legs, pressing against my center. Roland's palms brace flat against the wall, caging me in. "Either you're pissed I went out... or because you're conflicted over what we did. Which is it?"

I glare at him, my insides seething with an uncomfortable mix of disgust, anger, and lust. "I am *not* pissed about you going out. I don't care where you stick your dick. Not unless you have photos surface. Then I will be livid beyond measure. And conflicted?" I reach up and grab his throat, tightening my fingers enough to feel his blood pulsing through his veins. "Last time I checked, I came on to you and I'm the one who made *demands*. I'm pissed because you ran off like a scared little boy instead of talking to me."

His body presses into mine. The heat of his breath washes over me as he leans his mouth next to my ear. "Why *do* you care, Izzy?"

"Oh. Now it's Izzy again. Make up your mind, Roland. Are we friends or enemies? Because you need to decide."

His voice is husky as he murmurs, "Why not both?" One hand comes down off the sheetrock and skims my side, the tips of his fingers brushing beneath my shirt. I suck in a breath as he skates his hand up over my belly, coming to a rest on my breast. He squeezes the heavy mound, his thumb brushing across the lace covered nipple, making me squirm beneath his touch. I close my eyes and fight back the butterflies rolling in my stomach—we can't do this again...I *won't* be able to pick up the pieces he'll leave behind when he walks away... *again.*

Pleading softly, I murmur the only word I can force out, "Roland."

The door opens and I stiffen beneath him. "Oh *shit.* Sorry man—I didn't know you had someone in here. The guys are ready to go on again."

"I'll be there in a second." The door closes and I can't bear to open my eyes. The embarrassment of being caught like this, burns in the pit of my stomach, mingling with the churning nerves. "Look at me, Izzy." His finger continues its torture against my pert tip, making my body ignite with a fire I don't want to acknowledge.

When I finally crack them open, what I find leaves me breathless. His own Caribbean eyes burn with desire and want. Barely above a whisper, I barely manage to get out. "People are going to talk."

"Who fucking cares." His free hand tangles in my hair, holding me in place as his mouth crashes over mine, silencing the complaint. I don't want to like the feel of his lips on mine, but I can't deny it—not when the moan slips from my throat. Roland rips away, leaving me disheveled and confused as he reaches up to fix his hair. "We'll finish this tonight... at *home*."

He hurries from the room, leaving me more confused than ever. Righting my shirt, I dust my palms down my pants. Stalking toward the bathroom, I flick on the light and cringe when I see my reflection in the mirror. My once tame locks look like wildfire. The red tendrils are tangled and a mess. Turning on the water, I splash my face, trying to quell the blush staining my cheeks. I feel like I've been run ragged over the last four weeks, and my appearance, despite the hot encounter moments ago, reminds me of that.

Running my fingers through the tangles in my hair, I try to straighten the strands into the professional mask I need when I step out of here. Once I get them somewhat under control, I take a last glance at myself. My lips are swollen and the glow that kisses my skin will be impossible to hide from his bandmates, and I pray they won't ask questions. Hell—they *already* wonder why I'm staying with him at every stop on this tour. I guess now they'll just assume I'm fucking him to keep him from going elsewhere, which wouldn't be a bad idea if I could separate the sex from the complicated feelings churning inside. Taking a deep breath to stave the bile I feel burning inside, I push away from the sink. A wave of dizziness hits me, momentarily making me stagger. I'm in desperate need of sleep —*good* sleep. Something I've lacked since taking this job.

Me being in here with Roland will only add to the gossip. I suppose I should be grateful it's not more photos of him in some compromising position, instead. His reputation won't suffer from the rumor of us having an affair.

No... this time it'll be *my* reputation under fire.

# 8

# Roland

*Fuck.*

I shouldn't have kissed her. Truth be told, I've done a *lot* of things I shouldn't, yet kissing her after walking away from her in Chicago takes the cake. I couldn't bear to look at her after I locked myself in my room and cried like a petulant child. The way she took control had me harder than any woman at any of the clubs I've gone to—and that scared the shit out of me. And then, giving into temptation, I drove my steel rod into her core without a second thought about the consequences.

Pressing my fingertips to my lips, I still taste the sweetness of her Chapstick lingering on my mouth as I take the stage. The thump of the bass drum matches the rhythm of my heart... beating in tune with the desire still burning in my veins. I've never wanted a woman the way I want Izzy, and that scares the fuck out of me. I wasn't kidding when I told her I was the darkness, and I can't be the reason her light is snuffed out of existence. My past is a tangled web that still haunts me–hell, it'll forever haunt me. It's molded me into the fucked-up version my fans see. Someone like Izzy deserves a man who can face *his* demons and then slay hers—not give her more. It's part of why I walked away from her all those years ago. She didn't deserve the drama of my life then… and she doesn't deserve it now.

Somehow, I make it through the night without a hiccup and end my show. As soon as I'm offstage, I go in search of her. When my drummer catches up to me, I know what he's about to say.

"Don't ask, Mikey."

"What?" He throws his hands in the air in mock submission. "I was only going to say good for you. You can't go wrong with a woman like her."

"She's not mine."

He snickers. "Could have fooled me. I saw her look, and that was the look of a woman who's in love."

I blink at his words, confusion hitting me hard. "Love? Are you stupid? Izzy fucking despises me. What you saw was me trying to break her out of her cold-ass shell and maybe loosen that stick she has up her ass. Love? Nah—now lust? Maybe… I'd definitely tap that."

I swallow the disgust of my words as I turn away, shielding him from the truth I know is burning in my eyes as he murmurs, "Wouldn't we all, man? But you keep telling yourself that it's nothing, Roland. I see how she watches you when you're not looking. I don't know what's going on between the two of you, but it's more than a musician and PR manager. That woman is falling for you, even if she won't admit it herself."

"Impossible. The shit I've put her through isn't some lightweight shit, Mikey. If anything, she's more likely to want to cut off my cock and beat me with it. Besides, what you're probably seeing is the past we used to share—nothing more."

"Damn… can you be less graphic, man? My balls just shriveled inside me. But seriously… Isabella wants you, man. And your past might be exactly why it's so fucking hot between you. Anyway… that's not why I came over here, but that *you* think it is—that's more telling than anything. We're heading out for drinks since it's our last night here. You coming?"

I can't shake his words. The need to find Izzy is tenfold, so I shake my head no. "Nah… I'm supposed to meet up with my brothers. Have fun and stay out of the paparazzi's lens, ok? We can't handle any more of us winding up on the front page of the Enquirer."

"I don't think that's an issue, Winston. They're not after *us*. You're the one with some weird tastes that the media loves to gobble up. I'm pretty sure we're all safe as long as *you* keep fucking up."

Growling, I shove his shoulder from behind. "Fuck off."

Mikey laughs, as he shoots the bird over his shoulder, calling, "You first!" Before I can snarl a reply, he hurries off to meet up with the band. I hate ditching them, but I promised my brothers I'd meet them later and I won't break a promise to them. It's about all I'm good for these days. Pushing into my dressing room, I silently hope to find Izzy. Instead, it's empty. Yanking my cell phone from my back pocket, I swipe through the contacts and press her picture.

Her voice rasps through the line. "What?"

"Where'd you go, Freckles? I told you we'd pick up where we left off when I was done."

"The world doesn't revolve around you, Roland."

Her sudden distance makes me confused, and I rub my head. "Damn, Izzy. I thought you wanted this, finally?"

She sighs heavily into the phone. "I don't have time for your shit right now. I'm tired and not feeling well, Roland. I'll see you later.

But let's be real here… at least give me until tomorrow after I've slept before you come barging in, not taking 'no' as an answer."

Sick? I didn't notice anything earlier… of course I had my mind on *other* things. "What's wrong? Do you need me to bring you anything?"

The intake of breath tells me I've shocked her. "Wow, Roland. And here I thought you didn't have a caring bone in your body."

"Izzy… I know we've had our ups and downs—and maybe I've been a bit of a dick since Chicago."

Her bitter laugh cuts me off. "You *think?*"

"Look. I'm trying here, ok? You caught me by surprise…"

She snorts into the phone. "Fine. No, I don't need anything but sleep. Actually—I do. Along with staying out of my hair, stay out of the tabloids tonight. It's the least you can do. Goodnight, Roland."

The line goes dead, and I'm left staring at the blackened screen. "Fuck."

"Sorry to interrupt." I glance at the doorway. "…but I wasn't sure if you knew. Izzy left sick."

I nod my head at Liam, my head of security, as I squeeze the device in my hand and hold it up. I close my eyes and blow out a breath, grabbing my shit as I grumble, "I know. Can you run me home?"

We head towards the apartment building—and toward Izzy. "You ok, Roland?" Liam glances up in the rearview mirror. "Normally I try to stay out of your business—you have enough people telling you what to do, but…" He takes a breath, waiting for me to speak. When I arch a brow at him, he continues. "I'm worried about you. This version of you isn't who you really are. Aren't you tired of the bullshit?"

"Yeah—but it's all I know, Liam."

He shakes his head as we pull into the parking garage. "You're wrong about that. You know something better... you're just afraid to reach out and take it."

He doesn't say anything else as we climb from the car. Sending him to his apartment, I hurry inside and press the button for the Penthouse. Something in my gut is telling me something is going on with Izzy, and I need to check her. As soon as I walk inside, I know I'm right—she's not okay. I can hear her soft cries in her room, and not caring if I make her mad, I automatically move towards her door. Remembering I was supposed to meet my brothers, I pull my phone from my pocket and wake the screen to search for Drake's contact.

"Roland."

"Hey. Everything okay at the hospital?"

"Define okay. The judge's wife fell down the stairs and broke her arm. You still feel like grabbing a drink?"

As much as I can hear the desperation in his tone, I close my eyes and blow out a breath. "Can I get a raincheck? I'm beat and I have something I need to deal with."

"Yeah, okay. When are you back in Atlanta?"

"A few weeks. My last show is in Austin, then I'm in the studio for a couple of weeks."

When I push open the door, her sobs become louder, and the sound cuts me to the core.

"Roland, are you okay?"

I hesitate for a moment before answering my brother, guilt gnawing at my gut. "Yeah, I will be. I think. Sorry, look, I need to go. Tell Gage I'll catch up later."

"You'd tell me if you needed help, right?" The concern in his voice is clear.

"It's not like that, Drake, but I need to take care of this."

He groans into the line. I can tell he isn't buying my answer, but right now, I need to get to Izzy. "Yeah, okay. Call me this week. Be safe, Rol. Love you."

Stepping into her room, I'm gut punched by the sight of her laying on the bathroom floor. "Shit… Izzy."

Rushing to her side, I brush the hair away from her face. It's clear she passed out at some point from the position of her body near the toilet. A part of me worries about moving her, but I can't just leave her here, so I push that aside and slip my hands under her body to scoop her off the cool tile. Her head bobbles against me like she's lost control of her neck. Her body weighs nothing in my arms as I carry her to the bed, but what freaks me out the most is the lack of reaction from her.

"Freckles, can you tell me what happened?"

"Sick…" She groans as I slide her to the mattress and press my palm to her forehead. Izzy mumbles something about putting her down on the tile floor and leaving her to die, but I ignore her protests and tighten my hold on her. Pressing my hand to her head, I sigh in relief at her normalish feeling temperature.

"You don't feel like you have a fever. Maybe it was something you ate. Let's get you comfortable so you can rest."

I pull her shoes off her feet and toss them to the floor. Moving to the button on her pants, I hesitate for a second. For a moment, I wonder if she'll think this is taking advantage of her again, but one glance at her face and I say fuck it. She's completely out of it, which means she can't do it for herself. I can't stand to be in my clothes when I feel like shit–undressing her will make her feel better. At least that's what I keep telling myself as I strip her..

"I got you, Freckles."

I whisper into the quiet as I ease her slacks down her legs and toss them to the floor. She's wearing a simple cotton shirt, so I leave it on for *her* sake and to keep myself from slipping and attempting something she'll never forgive me for doing. Tugging the sheet over her body, I turn to leave, but the whimper that escapes her lips makes me halt in place.

Turning to face her, I can't look away from her still frame. It hits me like a lightning strike—I can't leave her alone tonight. Making a snap decision, I sprint to my room. Stripping my shirt over my head and kicking off my shoes, I move toward the shower. I can't climb into bed with her smelling like I just ran a marathon. Taking a deep breath, I shove my pants down, boxers and all, and toss my glasses to the counter before climbing into the stall. The cold water hits me like icicles, but my patience is thin—the need to be back in her room has me taking the fastest and *coldest* shower ever.

Rinsing the suds off, I step out and towel off. Not caring one bit about my nudity, I shove my specs onto my face and strut across the room to snatch some boxers from my drawer. Tugging them over my ass, I dart out of my bedroom and hurry back to hers. When I step inside, I inhale a breath as my eyes land on her still form. Her leg's untangled from the sheet and the shirt she's wearing has crept up her body, exposing the lacy panties she's wearing. Adjusting myself, I push down the feral need building and close the door.

Pulling back the cover opposite of her, I climb in and settle on my back. For some reason, leaving her so out of it when she's ill feels impossible. Forcing my eyes closed, I listen to her breaths and will myself to go to sleep. Izzy mumbles something in her sleep as her body shifts beneath the covers. My entire body stiffens, and my hands jerk into the air as she presses against me, her leg covering mine as she nestles into my side. My hands are frozen above me as her head burrows into the groove of my arm, but when she sighs against me, I give up and wrap it around her. Taking a deep breath, I catch the scent of gardenias and mint. It reminds me of a time that seems so long ago—a time that has been lost to me since I was a small boy. But the scary part... the part that makes me question everything is the way it calms me.

This—her close to me, is nothing I've ever felt before. Sex for me is about carnal pleasure and release. It's the closest I allow myself to women—and even then, it's with a strict set of rules. I've certainly never let one into my home, much less shared a bed. But holding her like this gives me a glimpse into a life I never thought I'd get close to having. And it makes me want for something I simply can't have.

Because no matter how she makes me feel... my demons will do nothing but drown her in the darkness.

# 9

# Izzy

My head pounds like Mikey is playing a riff against my temple. Stretching, I freeze at the solid mass I'm pressed against. Flattening my palm, I force open an eye and realize that the hard thing is Roland. My leg is tangled with his and my breasts, while covered in a shirt and bra, are pressed against his side. Moving my hand, I inadvertently brush the morning wood he's sporting and suck in a breath.

"Sweetheart, if you don't stop—I'm not going to be able to stay gentlemanly."

Snorting at his words, "You? A gentleman?" My hand stays pressed against his abdomen, just inches away from his cock. "Roland... why are you in my bed?"

"Not for the reason you're thinking. I came home last night because you didn't sound right on the phone. When I got here, you were passed out on the bathroom floor."

"And you what? Undressed me and put me to bed?"

"Pretty much." His fingers rub circles on my back as he continues to talk. "I took off your shoes and pants, then tucked you in. I was afraid to leave you alone, so I took a quick shower and slept in here. You were pretty sick last night, Izzy. I was worried."

"And how did we get into *this* position?"

Roland's hand tangles into my hair. The sensation is not something I should want or crave, but I lean into his hold more. "You rolled over and turned me into your personal heater. It's ok, though— it's… actually the first time… in a *long* time that I slept through the night."

"Oh." I tug my hand off his body and wiggle out from under his arm. I need space from him ASAP—his admission has me more confused than ever. "I need to use the bathroom."

Hurrying off before he can say anything else, I shut myself inside the ensuite and lean against the sink. Daring to look in the mirror, I cringe. My hair looks like a bird's nest and my skin is a lovely shade of pale. Turning on the water, I grab my toothbrush and load it up with toothpaste. Scrubbing my mouth to avoid the plethora of swear words burning against my tongue, I take my frustration out on my teeth. Finger combing through the tangles of my red hair, I take a deep breath and try to brace myself for the man who's probably still laying in my bed half-naked. Knowing I need to rip this off like a band-aid, I yank open the door.

"Rola—" I slam right into his firm chest. My breath whooshes out of me as he grabs my shoulder to steady me on my feet.

"I was worried about you."

Closing my eyes, I take a step back, which allows him to step inside the room with me. "You shouldn't be. I'm fine… as you can see. In fact, I think I'll take a shower."

"Good idea." He slams the door closed and shoves around me. I watch in confusion as he turns on the shower and turns toward me. "You passed out last night, Izzy. So, if *you're* showering, so am I."

"What? No. You can't shower with me, Roland. You already showered. And I'm fine. I think it was just me working too hard or something." I hop around on my feet like I'm doing an Irish jig. "See... perfectly capable of getting in alone." He ignores me. A devilish grin spreads across his face. I watch in shock as he uses my toothbrush. "Hey—that's *mine*."

He arches a brow as he spits out the toothpaste and rinses the brush under the water. "I think you've had my spit in your mouth already—it'll be fine, but if it bothers you that much, I'll replace it."

The clanking of the plastic against the holder jars me out of my trance. Growling in frustration, I put my hands at my sides and stomp my foot like a toddler who isn't getting her way.

"You *can't* shower with me."

"I can." He steps forward and turns on the water. "And I *will*." He pulls my shirt over my head, then reaches behind me and unfastens my bra. Roland jerks my panties down before I realize what's happening.. "I can carry you in... or you can walk, Izzy. Which is it?"

Mumbling a few choice words under my breath, I hurry into the glass stall and shove my head into the falling spray. Maybe he'll just leave—because having him in here with me means there's nowhere to run. Deep down, I don't really want to, but letting him in means taking a risk that will end in me heartbroken. Roland isn't like me. I realize that now. He was right to put space between us because I'll get attached and he'll walk away. He doesn't mean to, but he uses people to get what he wants, sealing his heart off to anyone who might get close. I don't. And the pound of the offending organ against my ribs reminds me I'm dangerously close to having it ripped out by the asshole... again.

"You're going to drown yourself if you stay like that." He gently tugs me back against his bare chest. Brushing the wet strands of hair from my eyes, I stare at the ceiling praying for strength. This man is going to be my death.

He's wearing his boxers still, keeping a barrier between us. "Roland... what are you doing?"

"Taking care of you."

"You don't take care of anyone... at least anyone who isn't one of your brothers."

He ignores me as he squeezes the body wash in his hand. "Maybe I can change."

"You..." An unintentional snort slips out. "Change?"

He lathers the creamy cleanser in his palms, then settles them on my bare shoulders. "Yeah... me. I don't know how to have a relationship, Izzy. But if I could—I'd want it with someone like you, again. Ok?"

I don't know what to say, so I don't speak. Instead, I close my eyes and count to ten as his calloused hands glide over my flesh, the suds leaving a trail of heat in their wake. He brushes his hand across the red curls covering my mound, but doesn't linger.

I whimper his name. "Roland." His hand stills against me. "What are you waiting for?"

"Izzy... just let me take care of you, ok?." Fighting back the tears, I nod, my head brushing his bare chest. "I'm sorry, Izzy. I never meant to hurt you. Not then... and not now."

"What—" my words die as he spins me to face him. The water rains down over him like he's some kind of God—but I know different.

He's no God… he's the fucking devil come to destroy me.

Roland presses his lips over mine, placing a chaste kiss against them before he tips my head back into the water. My eyes close at the sensation of him lathering my hair and rinsing it. I feel like I'm trapped in some alternate universe, and I'm afraid to be set free. This is the Roland I remember—the one I desperately want, but can't have.

Cutting off the water, he leads me out and wraps a towel around his waist and kicks off his wet boxers. He wraps me in the fluffy cotton and lifts me into his arms. He drips water across the floor, uncaring as he moves us onto the bed. Roland drops me on the mattress and slowly tugs the towel from my body. He climbs in beside me, kicking off his towel and tugging the covers over our frames.

I bite down on my lip and furrow my brows. "Roland, what are we doing?"

"Right this moment? I'm hoping to make love to you, Izzy."

My heart stops at his words, afraid to let them penetrate my own. But as he wedges himself between my thighs, I know it's too late. Trying to ignore the head of his cock poised at my entrance, I ask, the question burning on my lips.

"Is this a mistake?"

With a slow thrust of his hips, he buries himself inside me. His palm covers my cheek as he holds my gaze. As he brushes his thumb across my bottom lip, his eyes fill with an emotion I've never seen. "The only mistake was walking away from you all those years ago, Freckles."

He begins to move inside me. He's slow and deliberate—not demanding like before. This feels like something different... something scarier.

I arch my back, my breasts pressing into his chest. "Roland..."

"Don't think, Izzy. Just feel. I don't know what tomorrow will bring, but I know right now you're all I want." He rocks his hips, the tip of his shaft rubbing that sacred spot inside my core. His fingers find my jaw as he forces me to look at him. "I forgot how this feels—how *you* feel." Roland's mouth covers mine and his tongue pushes inside. He commands my body and soul perfectly, making me forget all about the reasons why this is a bad idea.

"You're going to break my heart, Roland." I whisper against his mouth.

His body stills for a moment as he looks into my eyes. "I can't break it if you don't give it to me, Izzy. Guard yourself from me— monsters don't deserve anyone's heart. I want to love you, but I can't. Not the way you deserve, and that guts me. But right now... in this moment I can make-believe my life wasn't filled with pain and torture. Right now... all I want to feel is you and me. Let go and let me make you feel like you're on fire... like I'm feeling when I'm with you, Freckles."

I force the tears down and nod my head. "Please, Roland..."

I lose myself to his magical touch. His fingers twine with mine and he pushes my hands above my head. He never misses a beat continuing the erotic tango we're trapped in. Nothing about this is right. I should hate him for what he's doing to me. As I stare into his eyes, his words playback—*Guard yourself from me. Monsters don't deserve anyone's heart. I can't love...* and like a red-hot poker, my insides burn from the strike against the one organ he doesn't want. And despite his warning, there's nothing I can do to guard myself... because, whether or not he wants my heart, it's already his.

He's not the man who will slay the monster under my bed.

He *is* the monster under my bed.

# 10

# Roland

My life is a shit storm of epic proportions. My brothers are caught up in some kind of trouble, and I'm stuck in Phoenix. After I got the call from some asshole, demanding I tell Gage to return his sister, I reached out to Archer. Apparently, Gage has gone to ground with a woman named Poppy. And Drake—fuck, I don't even know what to think about *him*. He's taken a judge's wife into protective custody. And from what Archer tells me, Drake has fallen for her.

Then there's *me*.

I'm tangled up with Izzy in ways I shouldn't be. She wants things I can't ever give her. Which is why I'm back to being the brooding asshole she hates. After spending the night in her arms back in Atlanta, then the epic morning we shared, I knew I needed to put some distance between us. I avoided her like the plague in New Orleans–another dick move, but I couldn't face her. After this show, we'll head back to Atlanta for two days before heading to Austin— the change in plans irritated me, but my manager insisted. He claimed we had to deal with a few things before heading to Austin, the last stop on my tour. I've holed myself up in the rented studio, praying for the music to distract me.

*We were perfect back when we were kids.*

*I close my eyes and wish for that time.*

*In my mind, that's where I keep you.*

*So, what are you doing with a man like me now?*

*It's you who wears that haunted Look,*

*When you should be wearing a gorgeous Smile,*

*I'm left dreaming about the day when you woke up in my arms.*

*When your arms held me tight, I felt peace for the first time.*


*So, this is me pleading,*

*Standing here begging, "Please don't go."*

*So, this is me pleading,*

*Standing here begging, "Please don't go."*


*I go back to your memory all the time.*

*It turns out freedom ain't nothing without you,*

*I'm left realizing I loved you.*

*But when I think of you…I know I'll always be a fool.*


*So, what are you waiting for?*

*Please, don't let me lose you again.*

*You were perfect. You're still perfect.*

*I'm the one that doesn't deserve you.*

*So, this is how it goes.*


*We were perfect back when we were kids.*

*I close my eyes and wish for that time.*

*In my mind, that's where I keep you.*

*So, what are you doing with a man like me now?*

*It's you who wears that haunted Look,*

*When you should be wearing a gorgeous Smile,*

*I'm left dreaming about the day when you woke up in my arms.*

*When your arms held me tight, I felt peace for the first time.*


*You were so beautiful, but I couldn't be saved by anyone*

*Your bright eyes told me what I had yet to discover.*

*It seemed only natural to put my heart and soul into your hands.*

*When you held me tight, it was a moment of peace I felt.*


*So, this is me pleading,*

*Standing here begging, "Please don't go."*

*So, this is me pleading,*

*Standing here begging, "Please don't go."*


*So, this is me pleading,*

*Standing here begging, "Please don't go."*

*So, this is me pleading,*

*Standing here begging, "Please don't go."*


*I go back to your memory all the time.*

*It turns out freedom ain't nothing without you,*

*I'm left realizing I loved you.*

*But when I think of you…I know I'll always be a fool.*


*I go back to your memory all the time.*

*It turns out freedom ain't nothing without you,*

*I'm left realizing I loved you.*

*But when I think of you…I know I'll always be a fool.*

I toss the pen I'm writing with and stare down at the lyrics. I'm royally fucked, and it's all because of a woman. Leaning my head back against the soft cushioned chair I'm in, I close my eyes and let my thoughts drift. Are me and my brothers this fucked up version of men because of the train wreck my dad left behind? Knowing this is doing nothing for my stress, I gather my shit and phone my driver. It's time to face the vixen and get some shit out in the open.

"Liam." I call out to my longtime bodyguard as I walk toward the car. "Let's go. I need to check on Izzy."

"Sir… if I may give you a piece of advice—don't hurt her. Izzy's different. She isn't like the ones you usually use and throw away."

Grunting at his fair assessment of me, I ignore him the rest of the short ride from the studio to our hotel. I've barely had time to come up with what I'm going to say, and it feels like whatever words I deliver—Izzy will reject them. And I can't blame her. It's been weeks since we crossed the invisible line in the sand and gave in to the desire. And only two weeks ago, I had her in my arms and made love to her. Something I've never done with *any* woman.

After dismissing Liam, I step into the penthouse and know things are not ok. Izzy is fast asleep on the couch, but even I can see she's been crying. "Izzy." I squat down in front of her and brush the strands of crimson hair from her face. "Sweetheart, did something happen?"

Her puffy eyes open and the reddened orbs of her once glittering eyes take me in. "Roland?" She pushes to a sitting position and blinks away the sleep. "What are you doing here? I thought you were at the studio working on music."

"I was... but I wanted to talk to you before tonight's show. Why have you been crying?"

She seems to hesitate but gives me a smile that barely reaches her eyes. "I watched a sad movie and must've fallen asleep." Her eyes cut toward the ensuite as she pushes herself to her feet. "I'll be back... I need to use the little girl's room."

I shift back, giving her room to make her escape, but my eyes stay glued to her like a fly in a spider's web—and despite the excuse she gave me, I can't help but wonder if there's something she's hiding.

A few minutes pass before she finally emerges from the bathroom. "Everything ok?" I move to the small kitchen and pull a bottle of water out of the refrigerator. Izzy slips onto a stool and snatches my drink.

"Yeah—fine." The movement of her throat as she chugs my water sends a bolt of desire straight to my loins. "What time do we need to be at the performance center?"

"Four."

"I need to shower." She tosses the empty plastic into the trash can and saunters toward her room.

The suite is divided into four parts—her room, my room, the shared bathroom that connects them, and the main living room consisting of the sitting area and small kitchen. I know I should go to my room, but like a magnet, she tugs me behind her.

"Izzy... what's going on?"

She ignores me as she heads into the bathroom, peeling her shirt off as she does. I want to be the good guy here, but seeing her strip is testing my limits. "Can you let me shower in peace, Roland?"

Like the last thread holding together my sanity, something inside me snaps. "No. I can't."

Grabbing her arms, I shove them above her head and slam her back against the closed door to my room. "I can't get you out of my system, Izzy. You've poisoned my veins and you're all I think about."

"I need you to go." Izzy shoves me back until I'm standing in her bedroom. "Boundaries, Roland. Learn some, ok?"

"Izzy. What's wrong?"

"What happened in Atlanta cannot happen again. It was a mistake."

She practically runs from the bathroom. "Wait." Chasing after her, I snag her wrist, halting her in place. "Talk to me Izzy. Are you mad at me because of what happened? Because I'm pretty sure you initiated it the first time. Come on—talk to me because right now I'm getting some pretty fucked up mixed signals."

"Yeah. That's the problem, Roland. Sometimes what we want isn't what we get. Sex between us is off the charts, but that's all it is— sex. I can't keep doing this with you, thinking one day you'll want more." I step toward her, but she puts her hand up. "Please. Don't make this harder than it should be. The tour is almost over, and your reputation seems to be intact...barely, but I digress."

"What are you saying?"

She looks at me and I can *feel* her pain. "I don't know... but my contract with the label was always supposed to be done at the end of the tour if we cleaned your image up."

Panic socks me in the gut and I can't shake the feeling she's going to leave. "Don't they want to be sure?"

"I'm sure. That's why when we are done here—we'll go back to Atlanta and meet with the label and my company. Until then, I'm asking you to keep this professional. I can't take any more heartache, Roland. I can't deal with the stress right now."

"What does that mean?"

She snorts as she waves her hand in the air. "Think you could let me shower? As enlightening as this conversation is, we have some-where to be."

"Fine... but we're going to talk about this, Izzy."

Spinning on my heel, I storm through the joined bathroom and slam the door behind me. If she thinks she's walking away from me —from us... she's wrong.

I let her go once in my life. I won't do it twice.

And I'll do anything I need to keep her here... *with* me, even if that means doing something *drastic*.

# 11

# Izzy

JUST AS EXPECTED, Roland has gone back to being the cold, heartless man he was when I was dropped into his lap months ago. I asked for it, so I don't know why his cool as a cucumber attitude has me pissed. We're currently back in Atlanta, sharing his apartment for two days before heading on to Austin. Pressing my hand under my ribs, I push down the anger and walk into his room to tell him both our managers have summoned us to the office. It's a meeting I know he's going to hate. We have one more show in Austin and after that... I'll hopefully be done. This relationship has evolved into something bordering torture for me. He's the one thing I want... but the one that must stay out of reach. And that hurts more than the loss of my parents years ago.

He's standing at the windows, staring at the city skyline. Roland is shirtless, giving me the perfect view of his lean, but muscular, back. My eyes travel the exposed skin as they drift down to the gray sweatpants hanging precariously off his hips. I have to force down a groan of pleasure from the mere sight of him. It's best if I keep him inside the box I've stuffed my feelings inside.

"Roland."

The subtle shift of his body lets me know he's heard me, but he doesn't turn around. "What?"

"Our bosses have requested our presence at the PR firm. We need to leave in thirty minutes."

"Fine. I'll meet you in the living room in ten minutes. I need to get dressed. Unless you want to help me with that—" He finally turns to face me, his fingers brushing the signature leather cuff he never takes off. "Then, by all means, stay."

Biting down on my lip to refrain from muttering the string of swear words gathering in my head, I turn and hurry out of his room. Another minute trapped in the space with him and one of us will combust. And I'm pretty sure it's going to be the type of combustion I've been working hard to avoid.

Waiting for his royal highness to get ready gives me time to think. I know we've almost wrapped up his touring schedule, which means I'm likely done for a bit—at least, that's what I'm hoping. My contract was only negotiated thru the end of his band's tour. And since Roland has miraculously managed to avoid the press, his manager seems to think he's changed the dynamic of the tabloids. He's avoided hitting their front page for *weeks*... I just hope it's enough, because I desperately need a break.

I'm so lost in my thoughts I don't hear him step behind me. Not until his hands brush my hair aside and his lips burn against the tender flesh below my ear. Jerking forward, I growl at the audacity of the moment.

"Seriously Roland? Don't."

He presses into me. "Izzy... stop fighting this—whatever it is between us. I've given you space. But damn Freckles, how long are you going to act like we aren't connected?"

Sliding off the stool and away from him, I fold my arms over my chest and glare at him. Despite the way he looks in his sweatpants and fitted tee, I can't do this with him. "You and I need different things, Roland. I want—no, *need* stability in the man I'm with. You're like a faulty fuse that's been lit. No one knows if it'll fizzle out or if it'll explode. I can't wait around and see."

"Jesus Christ, Izzy. You act like I'm asking for your hand in marriage. I just want to date and see where it goes."

My arms drop to my sides, and I sigh. "That's the thing Roland... I already know that seeing where it goes will lead to heartache and that's a chance I can't—no, won't take. Not now that—" I stop myself from saying more. Roland doesn't deserve an explanation. He's an overgrown child who happens to be a billionaire. Cutting ties with this entire disaster of a farce relationship is best... for everyone.

"Not now that, what? What were you going to say, Izzy?"

Roland starts toward me, but I grab my bag and dart to the door. "It doesn't matter. You're you and I'm me... there is no *'us'*. Let's go. Our managers are waiting."

Roland stews like a bull pacing the corral, but he gives me the silence I desperately need right now. I can't fathom how I let my life get so fucked up, but it is and there's not much I can do to change the course I'm on now. We wordlessly climb from the car and amble into the office, where both Harold and Alan, my boss, are seated at the massive glass table waiting.

"Miss Holiday, Mr. Winston. Thank you for joining us." Alan waves us toward some empty seats. "As you know, we need to discuss the continuation of our firm's contract. It was initially agreed that Miss Holiday would stay on as your Public Relations Manager through the tour and then we'd reassess. Well... that's why we're here today. There's only one more show left."

Roland isn't subtle as he tenses in the seat beside me, making me cut my eyes to him. His expression is pinched, bordering on anger as he listens to Harold speak. "Roland, you've managed to stay out of trouble for a while, but as I've told Alan here, I still have reservations about terminating a contract with his firm. It's only been a few months, and I've seen a positive change in you in that time, but what reassurances can you give me that you've changed for the better long term?"

"I can't. As you've pointed out many times, I'm just a spoiled rich playboy who can't settle down or commit to anything but my music. Now… if you'll excuse me, I have somewhere I'd rather be. *Miss Holiday,* I'll see you later. Who knows, maybe you'll finally be free of this shit show after Austin. I'll see you later at the penthouse."

I sit flabbergasted at his childish display and watch with rapt attention as Roland storms out of the meeting without any concern whatsoever. It isn't until Alan clears his throat that I turn from the empty doorway and catch both men staring at me with speculation and concern.

"Care to enlighten us on what the fuck *that* was about?" Harold grumbles with disdain dripping off his tongue. "He's a dick on a good day, but that was bad, even for him."

Shifting in my chair nervously, I take a deep breath. "Roland harbors some anger toward me. He has been pushing for us to try the fake dating thing, and I'm still refusing."

"Would it be so bad, Isabella?" Alan drums his fingers across the surface of the massive piece of glass separating us. The table does little to hide anything, so I'm certain both men can see my leg bouncing like it's a jackrabbit. "Maybe you should stay on after Austin—for a few more months. Make sure his reputation doesn't fall off the wayside again."

I lean forward and narrow my gaze on my boss. I want to tell him to shove it up his ass, but the truth they don't know is I've fallen in love with the spoiled rich kid again. As much as I want to cut ties, I don't want to see him fall off the wagon, so to speak, again. "This was only supposed to be through the end of his tour. Well… after Austin, it'll be done. But I won't walk away. I fear it's going to take something big to make Roland grow up—and I worry about what that means for his image. But I can't continue the way we are. I'll stay on, but not from his penthouse. I'm sorry. I'm not willing to jeopardize myself and continue down this path."

"*Shit*." Alan leans back in his seat, his expression knowing. "You've gone and fallen for the client."

Rolling my eyes, I retort, "No, I've gone and fucked your client." I sigh as I instantly regret my words, but the damage is done.

Harold looks between us, his eyes landing on me. "Seriously? But you refused to be his fake girlfriend. If all *that's* been going on, why wouldn't you go along with the plan?"

"There's something I should have mentioned from the get-go. Roland and I grew up together… even dated through high school. We've got history together. And while I won't entertain your judgment of our relationship currently, I'll say this. He and I want different things right now. Me staying could eventually hurt his career and reputation. I'm asking you to honor my wish to move out of his house and continue like a *normal* manager would—from the office."

Harold purses his lips as he rests his hand on his portly belly, and he stares at me. I feel like he knows something more, but I pray it's just my nerves talking. "Fine. I want four more weeks, then we will re-evaluate."

I can handle four more weeks by simply avoiding him — unless I need to handle an issue. It'll be easy to do, living in my own house.

But anything beyond that and the train wreck I'm trying to avoid will derail. "We can come back here, and I'll stay at my place or a hotel if I'm needed elsewhere. Four weeks, and then we can reassess his image. If he's still maintaining the trend we're seeing now, we can shift to me being on retainer. I might be the best at managing snowstorms of drama when it comes to celebrities' lives, but it's getting to the point where I'll be the blizzard blowing through Roland Winston's life if something doesn't change. And neither of us needs that now or *ever*. This change is for the best—for everyone involved."

Harold seems to mull over my words before he nods his head in agreement. "Four weeks it is. Let's hope he doesn't do anything stupid in that time because the label is at their wit's end."

"Please. Ruger Records has dealt with far worse than the likes of Roland Winston. But I was dead serious when I said he needed to see someone about his issues. If you want me to stay on, he's got to talk to someone. This is something deeper than any of us can handle."

I push to my feet, pausing to glance at Alan. "I'll be taking some time off if everything goes well over the next four weeks."

Not waiting for his answer, I leave the conference room. Several of the employees are milling around, gawking at me as I wait for the elevator. I just want to get the hell out of here—the migraine that's skating at the edges of my vision is threatening to become more than I want to deal with today.

"Izzy?"

Cutting my eyes to the left, I spot Candice, the one person in this office I consider a friend. We're two of three women working for Axel Public Relations. The other female is a total bitch. She threw a huge hissy fit when she heard I got Roland's assignment. I guess sucking all the upper management's dicks didn't work out for her like she expected. It didn't help that Alan hates her guts—not to mention his wife would rather she be fired. He wouldn't have considered giving her this job. I shudder, thinking that *she* could be the one in my shoes right now. Roland would be royally fucked.

"Hey, Candice."

She tilts her head and narrows her gaze on me. "Have you lost weight? What are you doing differently?"

"Besides exhaustion?" I press the elevator button again as if it'll make the metal box appear faster. "Not a damn thing. Praying that after this music tour, I'll be able to take some time off. I'm worn out."

She snorts and leans against the wall. "You mean the pretty boy rockstar is a pain in the ass? I'm shocked." Candice feigns a shocked expression. "Hey, if he drives you too crazy, we can always run away for a while. I have a great condo just waiting for a girl's trip. But seriously... that's not what I'm referring to. You look... *holy shit*. You slept with him. I recognize the *'I've been fucked so good I'm dead on my feet'* look."

"Shhh... keep your voice down. We didn't do anything." Feeling guilty, I quickly add, "Last night. Look—" Glancing around, I scan the office space ensuring no one on the floor is in earshot to have heard her raunchy remark. "Roland and I have a *history*. We grew up together and dated throughout high school. Which has made this business partnership... *complicated*."

"What aren't you telling me? You know you can talk to me." Candice and I grew close after I started working here. She's older than me and kind of feels like an older sister to me. It's been hell being cut off from her these last few months, but Roland has literally taken all of my time. "My husband says that's one of my best traits." She smiles at me as we wait for the elevator to arrive.

A wave of dizziness hits me, and I steady myself against the wall just as the doors ping, announcing their arrival. Candice grabs my arm. "Ok... that's it. You're telling me what's going on, because I think it's more than dealing with someone who acts like a petulant man-child on a good day. I'm not buying this 'I'm just exhausted' bullshit. You've lost a lot of weight, Izzy, and your color is off. Come on—we can talk in the elevator."

Allowing her to pull me into the metal prison, I blow out a breath and lean against the cool wall and close my eyes.

"Spit it out, Izzy. Why do you look like you're about to pass out? Are you sick?"

Peeling my lids open, I shake my head and take a deep breath. Candice is watching me with concern. I don't have any siblings, and my parents have both passed, leaving me alone in this world of turbulent dealings. For the first time in weeks, I feel like I need to tell someone what's going on, and Candice is the only friend I have.

"Candice..." I fight back the bile burning in my throat. "I'm in trouble."

# 12

# Roland

FUCK THEM. *All* of them.

If Izzy thinks she's leaving because the tour is done—she's wrong. I'm not letting her walk away now, or ever. And if it takes me fucking up to make the label keep her on longer, well… I know exactly how to do just that.

I didn't even go home. I came straight here.

Club Vibe.

Maybe I'll luck out and hit the tabloids by morning. Then Izzy will have to stay on as my PR Manager. Then, I can convince her she belongs to me.

Dalton, head of security, nods in greeting as I step into the main room. Though I'm not dressed in the typical fashion of the club, my money is spent well here, so they won't dare say anything about my attire.

My eyes settle on a woman who's a known Domme. I'm pretty sure she's a switch and has done scenes with my brother Drake, but I don't give a fuck—I need to blow off steam and she's as good as any of them.

"Winston." She gives me a once over. "Interesting attire. Was this a spur-of-the-moment decision?"

Glancing down at my casual pants, I smirk. "Easier to come off."

She runs her long red nail down my chest. "Aww… are you in need of a scene tonight?"

Grabbing her hip, I pull her against my chest. "Kat, I'm in need of pain—nothing more. Can you do that for me?"

Wordlessly, she grabs my cotton shirt and leads me through the main room and down the hallway. Shoving open one of the private rooms, she tugs me inside like a dog on a leash. "What kind of pain do you want tonight, Winston?"

"Enough to make me forget."

She pauses, glancing over her shoulder at me as she smirks. "You know what I do—right?"

Holding her gaze, I shrug. "I know you've done scenes with my brother, but beyond that… no. Aren't you a switch?"

"Yes… but when I'm in control, it's pain I inflict—not pleasure."

"Works for me. I know my safe word."

She cocks her eyebrow and smirks. "Good. Get undressed and stand over there."

My body shudders from what she's pointing at, but I hide my reaction. There isn't much I won't do, except a dude—last time was close enough for me. But this… I strip my clothes off nervously, watching her out of the corner of my eye. Her stilettos clack against the hardwood floor, making my pulse skyrocket. This might be the hardest I've gone when it comes to painful stimulation.

Standing completely nude, my breath hitches when Kat steps beside me and cuffs my hands in leather restraints. Tugging the chain that connects them, she pulls me toward the wall where a series of hooks are embedded into the studs. Lifting my arms, she laces my cuffs over one and pats my side.

"Good boy. Now tell me… what's your safe word?"

"Red, Mistress."

"I'm not your mistress… in this room, when I wield your punishment—call me Madame. Understand, Winston?"

"Yes, Madame."

She kicks my feet apart, exposing my family jewels in a way that would leave most men embarrassed. It's not that I'm concerned about what I have to offer, because I was blessed with a healthy sized cock—it's the dangling, freeballing that's happening as I wait. My eyes widen slightly when she unfurls the black leather she's holding in her hand.

"I'll start off slowly—until you're warmed up and tolerating the way it feels against your skin." She flicks her wrist, making the coiled rope snap in the air. "Have you ever been whipped before, Winston?"

"No, Madame. Just paddles or floggers. Will this mark my skin?"

"Is that a hard limit?"

I think about it for a moment and shake my head no. "Maybe don't make me bleed… otherwise, do your worst."

"Oh… silly boy. You can't handle my worst if you don't want blood involved."

There was no amount of psyching myself up to prepare for the first lick of leather against my exposed flesh. I hiss out, but she doesn't give me any time to prepare for the next one and I gasp. Closing my eyes, I give myself over to the pain, letting it wash away the bitterness I have burrowed deep. I want to be normal—want things I don't know how to have. Each crack of the whip sizzles across my body. The burn is almost unbearable, but the release it's giving me is unlike anything I've done before.

"What the *fuck*?" Kat's voice jars me from the euphoric state I'm under.

Following her line of sight, I'm stunned to see a woman standing at the threshold of the door. Kat moves quickly, grabbing her by the arm and dragging her all the way inside the room. She tosses the redhead onto the bed and moves toward me, her eyes never leaving the woman.

"Don't fucking move."

Kat uncuffs me, the prickles of sensation slowly moving down my arms as I shake them out. Grabbing my discarded pants, I tug them on, trying to salvage some kind of dignity.

"Who the fuck are you, and how did you get in here?" I bark, making her cower in fear.

Her gaze flicks between Kat and me as she twists her hands nervously in her lap. "I… um. I'm Sabrina Stone. I work here."

"You *work* here?" I narrow my gaze on her, trying to assess what her game is. "And you thought what? You'd come in here and watch something you clearly weren't invited to participate in?"

"Didn't you notice the red light outside the door?" Kat moves closer. "It's there for a reason. To let other patrons, know, this is a private scene."

The traffic light system is one of many features the club has to keep patrons safe. Red means the room is closed to others as it's a private scene. Green is for those that don't mind participants joining in and yellow means voyeurs welcomed to watch. Obviously, this girl is new …or she just didn't give a fuck.

"What the hell is this?" Kat snatches the device hanging partially out of her pocket. "Were you going to take photos? Holy shit, Winston." She spins toward me, holding up the cell phone. "This bitch planned on videoing or taking pictures of us."

"Please… I didn't take any or record you. I'm sorry—I'll… I'll just go."

"*No, you won't.*"

Fury like nothing courses through my veins as I grab Sabrina by the arm. Dragging her toward the door, I shove it open and practically drag her down the hallway. Dalton spots me, his eyes wide with concern as he rushes to meet me halfway.

"Winston—what the fuck are you doing?"

"This *employee* interrupted my scene with Kat. She had her phone, Dalton."

Dalton stiffens. "You work here?"

Sabrina nods, "Yes, sir. I've been here for about six months. I'm s— sorry." Her voice cracks as she meets his gaze. "I didn't take any photos… I swear."

"Photos?" Dalton flicks his eyes between us. "What's she talking about?"

"Here." Kat thrusts the phone she's holding toward him. "This is hers. She had it in her pocket. She completely ignored the light on the door and barged in. I don't know how long she was standing there before I noticed her. She could have taken several photos before I realized."

Dalton takes it and presses a few keys on the screen. "Unlock it." He holds it out to Sabrina. When she hesitates, I stiffen. "I said *open* it—now. Or you won't like the consequences."

She reaches out with a shaky hand and keys in the passcode. "I promise I didn't take any photos tonight."

"Tonight?" I jerk her to face me. Shaking her slightly. "What do you mean, *tonight?*"

Dalton pulls her from my grasp. Stepping between us he pins me with a glare. "Go to Dom's office. I'll meet you two there."

He storms off, pulling Sabrina behind him. "Fuck." I scream the word as I pad barefoot down the hallway to the back where Dom's business office is. I imagine he's going to find Dom and loop him in on this mess. If this is the person who's been leaking photos of me to the media, I'll fucking destroy her.

Pushing open the door, I plop down on the couch. Dropping my head into my hands, I rest my elbows on my knees and blow out a frustrated sigh. I hadn't noticed that Kat didn't follow me, so when she steps inside and drops my shoes and shirt on the floor at my bare feet, I glance up.

"Here." She thrusts my cell phone at me. "It was on the floor in the room. I imagine you have someone you need to call."

Fuck. I hadn't even thought about the fact that I need to call Izzy. While I wanted to create a mess to make her stay, this feels ten times worse than I planned. Not to mention I don't really want her to see me inside the club. Pictures are one thing, but seeing it in person is a whole different story.

Waking my screen, I hover over her number. Hesitating, I call Drake instead.

"Roland." His voice is clipped as he answers. "What's up?"

Something is wrong. I can hear in his tone. "Drake… what's wrong?"

"Everything, Roland. Everything. But I don't want you involved in my mess. Are you ok? No more calls from Hugo?"

"Wait—is Gage ok? Is that why you're asking?"

"He's… fine." Drake's hesitation causes my skin to prickle. "Look-- if you're ok I need to go. Rhiannon needs me."

"Yeah. I'm good. Call me if you need me, brother."

Disconnecting the call, a sense of dread settles in my stomach. I know Drake helped Rhiannon get away from her asshole husband and Gage is somewhere in hiding with Alessandro Hugo's sister. But sitting here in my own mess—I can't help thinking they're keeping something more from me. Shaking my head, I make the call I dread.

"What do you want?"

Closing my eyes, I take a deep breath. "I fucked up, Izzy. I need you to meet me at Club Vibe. How soon can you be here?"

"Jesus Christ. I knew your choir boy streak was too good to be true. Lucky for you, I'm close by. I was busy handling another… issue. I'll be there in fifteen minutes."

Staring at the blackened screen, I realize now this was the worst thing I could do to get her attention. It's definitely not showing her I want to change.

"Are you going to sit there and sulk?" Kat's voice purrs across the room. "I take it whoever you called wasn't happy."

"You could say that." I lift my head and look over at her. "My public relations manager."

"Ouch." She winces. "Let me guess... you're supposed to be cleaning up your image, not here being a naughty boy."

Shrugging my shoulder, I lean back in the seat and close my eyes. How in the hell am I supposed to make this better? My brothers are tangled up in their own problems, which means they won't be able to bail me out of this mess. Not this time. Thoughts race around in my head, and I practically jump when the door opens.

"Winston." Dalton steps in and waves Izzy in behind him. "Found your woman at the entrance. You call her?"

"She's not my woman." The words are bitter tasting on my tongue. "She's my *PR* manager."

Dalton glances back at her. "If you say so. I've got Miss Stone with Dom in the employee lounge. It'll be a few more minutes."

He slams the door, leaving me to face off with Izzy, who is glaring at me like she wants to set fire to my balls. If she only knew how much I already burn for her, she'd laugh. Because sitting shirtless with another woman half-dressed clearly tells her something different.

"What the *fuck*, Roland?"

# 13

*Izzy*

I WORRIED he couldn't keep his shit together… but the same day we meet with our managers? *Fuck*. When he called and said he needed me at Club Vibe, I wanted to scream at him—but here I am, driving through the streets of Atlanta to do my job. The one I'm damn good at. I'm mad as hell at him, but I don't want his career to suffer—not when I know what's causing this side of him. I park my car and sit behind the wheel for a second. I've never been inside this prestigious sex club, despite growing up here and living fairly close.

Climbing from my car, I lock up and hustle inside. The entrance is vastly different from the exterior. While the outside has a warehouse vibe, the inside is like stepping inside the Fox Theater. Its dim lighting makes the red decor pop like something out of a 1950s gangster movie. The girl behind the counter eyes me, scanning my completely out-of-place attire.

"Can I help you?"

Shaking my head, I step up to the counter. "Yes. I need to speak with Roland Winston. He called me and asked me to meet him here."

"I'm sorry, but I can't give out member information—including whether they're here or not."

Growling in frustration. "Look lady. I don't want to be here at dinner time either—but Roland called me." Fishing out my phone, I flash her Roland's name and that was the last call I answered. "See. Now, if you would, please go get him."

"Honey—anyone can name a contact whatever they want."

A large man with skin the color of milk chocolate steps through a door behind her. He's massive and, well... gorgeous. "What's going on, Casey?"

"This woman is demanding to see a member. I refused to confirm if he was here and she's refusing to leave."

"Ma'am. I'm Henry Dalton, head of security—did you say Mr. Winston contacted you?"

"Yes. I'm Isabella Holiday—his public relations manager... and he's apparently gotten himself into some trouble."

Mr. Dalton grumbles something under his breath and then pushes open the small half-wall separating us. "Come with me."

Giving the woman at the counter a smug *told you so* look, I push around her and follow him into the club. A few people are milling around, and I can't help noticing their scantily clad attire. Averting my eyes, I follow Mr. Dalton down a dark hallway.

"Mr. Dalton, what exactly has he done this time?"

"Miss Holiday, please call me Dalton. And he hasn't done anything wrong—actually, an employee of ours is in trouble."

"Right… because him being here when I thought he was changing his MO isn't trouble at all."

Dalton shoots me a knowing look but doesn't say anything. "Here." He pushes open the door. "Winston." Dalton steps in, and waves me in behind him. "Found your woman at the entrance. You called her?"

"She's not my woman." He scrunches his expression as he avoids looking at me. "She's my *PR* manager."

Dalton glances back at me. "If you say so. I've got Miss Stone with Dom in the employee lounge. It'll be a few more minutes."

He slams the door and I'm left staring at the man I want to strangle. My heart hammers in my chest because he's sitting shirtless in a chair with his head down. Red marks crisscross his skin, but the part that has me fuming like a volcano ready to explode is the half-dressed woman sitting across from him. I shouldn't feel jealous, but seeing her tells me exactly what he was doing here this evening. And it's like a stake to the remaining bits of my heart.

"What the *fuck*, Roland?"

Roland's head snaps up, and he pins me with a look that leaves me choking back my anger. "I fucked up, Izzy. I came here tonight because I didn't want you to leave."

"Right… because having sex with another woman makes me want to stay?"

His eyes close and he blows out a breath. "I didn't have sex with her."

"Doesn't matter. You're here and you promised you would stop this shit, Roland. And you know what's comical? I *wasn't* leaving. The label asked me to stay on for four more weeks to ensure your good behavior continued. Guess the joke's on them because it took you less than two hours to fuck it all up again."

Before he can answer, a man who I assume is the owner strolls into the room. "Mr. Winston."

"Dom. Where is she?"

"Where is *who*?" I glance between the two men. "Someone tell me what the fuck is going on right now. Because as far as I can tell, Roland and this woman were doing some kinky sex act and something *bad* happened."

"And you are?" The man he called Dom glances at me.

"Dom… this is Isabella Holiday—my PR manager."

He steps closer to me, extending his hand. "Miss Holiday. I'm Dom —Vibe's owner. If you'll have a seat, I'll explain everything." He waves to the empty spot beside Roland, and I reluctantly sit down. "During a scene between Mr. Winston and Miss Pollard, an employee broke protocol and entered the room."

"A scene." I mumble, my fingers balling into a fist against my leg. "Is *that* what you call it?"

Dom holds his gaze on me a moment before making a clicking noise with his tongue. "Yes. Miss Holiday, what do you know about the lifestyle?"

"Only what I've seen in Fifty Shades of Grey." I snort. "And from the images, I've already attempted to clean up for Roland."

"I see. Well, the lifestyle has been incentivized for the big screen, but I can assure you it's more than that. Regardless, the employee entered a private playroom with the intent to photograph Mr. Winston."

I straighten against the plush cushions, the movement pushing me against Roland. "Is this the person who's been leaking photos the whole time?"

"We don't believe so. As far as I know, this club was not involved with the last photos that hit the tabloids and you can be sure we'll be increasing our security to maintain our clients' *privacy*."

Dom struts across the room and whispers something in the woman's ear. She smiles up at him as her long nail traces down his chest. She stands and moves in front of Roland and me. "Winston… It's been fun." She leans down and presses a chaste kiss to his cheek. "Hit me up if you want to continue the punishment later."

I watch as she saunters out of the room. "*Seriously?*" I glare at Roland. "Where is she going? We'll need her statement to press charges."

"You won't be pressing charges." Dom leans against his desk. "I'd like you to allow me to handle this… and dole out punishment as I see fit."

"You mean like prison? Because that's where she belongs. I want to talk to her."

Dom tips his head toward Dalton. "Go get her."

Dalton hesitates for a moment. "Is… is that a good idea?"

"Yes. Bring her in here so she can see what she's facing with her poor decision."

Dalton exits the room, leaving me completely confused. "How exactly are you going to punish her? And how does that fix *this*—" I wave my hand down Roland's frame. "…fucking disaster?"

"The thing is," Dom pauses. "…if this gets out, both of our reputations will be destroyed. I've sacrificed a lot to have my business, and I can't risk that. Since the photos never went anywhere—I'm hoping we can come to an agreement that leaves the police *and* media out of this."

"Yes." Roland finally speaks up beside me. "Whatever it takes to keep this under wraps. I don't need it getting out or the label finding out."

"You expect me not to *tell* them? That you were three presses of a button on a cell phone from a media shitstorm?" I look at him, ignoring the door that's opened. "What the fuck, Roland. Haven't we kept enough from them already?"

*"Please, Izzy."*

The clearing of Dom's throat has me turning around to face the newcomer. Dalton is leaning against the door with his arms folded across his chest and a woman stands in front of him. She's breathtakingly beautiful—but her eyes are filled with such sorrow I can't help feeling slightly sorry for her.

"This is Sabrina Stone—the employee in question."

Pushing aside the confusing sympathy for her, I snap. "*So.* You're the person leaking photos to the media. Why? Money?"

She shifts on her feet and swallows. "This is the first time I've attempted anything like this. But it doesn't matter anyway, does it? What's done is done, and I'm royally fucked. But I *am* sorry I caused all this trouble."

"Why'd you do it?" Roland questions her. "Did I do something to you, or was this all to get a fat paycheck?"

She blinks back the tears threatening to fall and sniffs loudly. "Why does it matter? I'm screwed, no matter what. I'd rather keep my reasons to myself, if you don't mind."

Growling under my breath, I can feel my anger about to explode. I shake my head, throwing both hands in the air, pinning Roland and then Dom with a glare. "Fine… whatever. You two do whatever the fuck you want, but count me out. I won't be part of it. I'm done." Standing from the couch, I turn to Roland. "This is low… even for *you*."

Turning. I push around Miss Stone and jerk the door open. Dalton grabs the frame, holding it open for me. "I'll walk you out."

Nodding, I let him follow me through the club. He escorts me all the way to my car, where he pauses. "Miss Holiday." His finger grips the driver's door. "I know you're pissed, but people come here for all different reasons. Dom is right. Hollywood has given people a false sense of what this lifestyle can be like. Roland has a lot of demons, and the club lets him get them out without fear of being ridiculed… or doing something *dangerous*. Well, he *used* to, until this shit started happening. I see how he looks at you. Be sure you're making the right decision before you run."

"How do you know what I'm going to do? You don't know me."

"No… but I know the look on your face. I've seen it on my own before. Don't live with regret like I do. It'll only hurt you in the end."

I scoff at his words. "You're wrong. Roland is the only one who can hurt me—rather, *has* hurt me. And keep on doing it. I don't know what you went through, but it's not the same."

"Yeah—true. But I gave up on someone because it was too hard to face the reality. Don't let that be you or you'll end up alone like me."

"Funny." I crank the engine. "You don't have to worry about me. Despite my feelings on a personal level, I'll do my job because even as angry as I am—I agreed to protect him. I've got to go, Dalton. Thanks for walking me out."

Jerking the door out of his grasp, I slam it shut. Careful not to back over him, I practically peal out of the parking lot. I've got to get out of here—because seeing Roland in his place after this is not something I want to do. Making a snap decision, I dial my boss on Bluetooth from the car.

"Isabella—everything ok?"

"No. Alan, I'm calling to tell you I am going to need to work remotely for a while. I need to take care of some personal issues. If that's not possible, I'll tender my resignation."

"Isabella… talk to me—what happened? Is it Winston?"

"Nothing I didn't ask for, Alan. Don't worry, it's not anything that will hurt the company. I promise I can handle his career without needing to be with him 24/7. Can you do me a favor? Can you just tell him I quit, and that the PR firm will hand over everything to someone else? He doesn't need to know I'm still working for him. In fact, I'd rather he didn't. If you could have all my things moved out of his apartment and back to mine. There isn't much there— just some clothes and things. I'm leaving tonight and won't have time to grab everything."

"Fine. I'll get everything taken care of and call Harold and let him know the change. Hopefully, they'll go for it."

If they don't agree—I'll quit. I don't give a shit. Pulling into my townhouse, I park and hurry inside. I don't have much time, and the only saving grace is Roland doesn't know where I actually live. At least, not yet, but I'm too smart to believe he won't track me down. Grabbing down another one of my suitcases, I fill it with clothes. I'll grab anything else I need once I get to my destination— seeing as all my toiletries are at his penthouse. Wheeling the bag down the steps, I hurtle it into the trunk and climb back into the driver's seat. Scrolling through the phone, I pull up Candice's number.

"Isabella… are you alright?"

I grimace when I see it's nearly nine at night. "Yeah… sorry to be calling so late, but you remember that offer for a girl's trip? Any chance you were serious?"

"Yeah… did something happen?"

Grunting, a half laugh, "You could say that. Look—I don't want to talk about it right now, but I need to leave town. Alan has agreed to let me work remotely for a while on the downlow. Everything will come through you from here on out. I just need to create some separation from Roland for a bit. I'd like to take you up and head down tonight, if possible."

Her sigh carries through my Bluetooth speaker. "Of course. I just texted you the address and door code. I assume *he* doesn't know about the change."

"No. And I don't really care. He doesn't have a say any more about what I do."

# 14

# Roland

"WHAT DO YOU MEAN, she's *quit*?"

I pace my penthouse floor like a cat on a hot tin roof. As soon as I walked through the door last night, I knew something was wrong—Izzy wasn't here. Security informed me she never came back, either. When I hurried down to the parking garage, I wasn't surprised to find her car wasn't there either.

"Exactly what it sounds like I'm saying." Harold grunts. "I don't know what the fuck happened, Roland, but you can't afford a fuck up with her gone. I don't care if Alan says her partner at the firm is just as good—we can't take that chance."

My phone chimes with an incoming call and I sigh heavily. "I need to call you back. My brother is calling."

Clicking off from Harold without waiting for a response, I try to disguise the panic in my own voice. "Drake—what's up?"

"Roland." He sounds broken as he says my name. It's not something I've heard in his voice since—he cuts my thoughts short. "Something's happened."

Bracing my hand against the counter, I barely manage to spit the word out, "Gage?" I mentally prepare for him to tell me Gage is gone.

"No—he's, uh, still MIA. It's Rhiannon. She… she—fuck, Roland, I can't lose her."

Shaken by his words, I gasp. "*Lose* her? Drake, what are you talking about? You're not making any sense."

His voice sounds almost faraway and wistful as he responds, "Our whole life has been a lie, Roland. Love exists—we just never got a chance to experience it. At least… until now."

It takes me a minute to put two and two together, but I realize he's talking about himself. "Who is she?"

"The judge's wife—I've fallen in love with her and broken every damn rule I set for myself. She came in and destroyed every wall I erected around my heart. You know me, Rols—I've spent a lifetime rejecting a woman wanting a relationship. But this is…different. This is…" He inhales loudly. "I can't lose her."

Shaking my head, even though he can't see me, I pry for information, "Help me understand, big brother. Why would you lose her? And isn't she still married?"

"He's going to jail for this…"

Drake is talking in circles and for the first time, I'm scared of him. Whatever is going on with the Judge's wife has him all tangled in knots—much like me and Izzy. Even thinking her name causes my heart to clench in pain. "Drake? I don't understand."

"No, you wouldn't. I tried to shield you, Rols… you were just a baby. But the things you saw—and heard fucked with your head. I know that, because it fucked with mine. And I'm sorry, *so* sorry, you had to witness it all. That wasn't real love… it was ownership.

What our parents shared was so fucking wrong. There's no way our father would've ever hurt mom the way he did if he felt half of what I feel right now. And now, it could all be over before I've even had a chance to tell her I love her."

"Why Drake? Just go and tell her."

"I can't."

"Fuck, brother. I don't know what's happened, but you can tell her —you *should*."

"I'm at Grady. She's in surgery, Roland. Rhiannon might not live through it. That monster hung her from the ceiling, trying to kill her. She fought him—God, her body was so battered. When we found her, she was... *fuck*." He growls. "She wasn't breathing. I don't... I don't know if I can survive this, Roland. If she dies.... I gotta go... I'll call you when I know something."

I stare at the phone in my hand like it's going to do something. The blackened screen feels like an omen of something bad to come, but I push it aside and call Harold back.

"Everything alright?" He grumbles into the phone.

"No, everything is not ok. I need to cancel the Austin concert. Something's happened and I need to get to the hospital."

"You can't be serious, Roland. *Cancel* the concert? Do you hear yourself? That will be career suicide—more than any dirty photo could ever be."

Mulling over his words, I realize I don't care. First Izzy left me, and now my brother is in trouble. "Then postpone it. I don't care. My brother's girlfriend is in the hospital and he's all alone because my older brother is tangled up in some cluster fuck with his woman. I won't let him sit there waiting to find out if she lives or dies. Either postpone it for a few months or cancel it—

either way, I don't care. Now do what I pay you to do and clear this shit up."

"You'll need to come to the studio and meet with the executives. They aren't going to take this from me, so you're going to need to come here and make your case. Because even I can't work a fucking miracle, Roland."

"Fine. I'll be there in an hour."

Changing my clothes, I call Liam. He drives us toward the studio, his eyes filled with concern, though he remains silent. "Just ask me, Liam."

"Is this about Miss Holiday?"

"No. My brother is at Grady—waiting to hear if his girlfriend is going to live or die. Her soon-to-be ex-husband tried to kill her and it's not looking good. Canceling the concert is the right move. There aren't many things that mean more than my music, but my brothers do."

"And Izzy?" He arches a brow—Liam sees more than he lets on, so I can only guess he's known longer than me how I feel about her.

"Yeah—and Izzy. But she'll have to wait for now. Hey, can you do me a favor while I chat with the big bosses?"

"Of course." He smiles at me.

Liam is like family to me—because, with the closeness of him being my bodyguard for the last six years, he's become like another brother to me. He'll do anything he can to help me out. Anything legal, anyway. Which means my request is something Liam *will* do, even if he doesn't agree.

"I need you to find out where Miss Holiday has gone."

The car stops, and as I climb out, Liam calls out to me. "You've fallen for her, haven't you?"

"I don't know, Liam. I don't exactly have anything to base it off of—and I won't know until she's back here where she belongs. Give me thirty minutes, then we'll head over to Grady. Family is more important than anything, Liam. *This* is just a formality."

As expected, the higher-ups weren't thrilled with my decision to cancel the concert, but they knew there was no stopping me. After some deliberation, we came to a mutual agreement to push the Austin date to three months. The venue was more than happy to accommodate, and it means no lost profits from refunded tickets. Harold agreed to make some calls to the Axel PR group and see if Alan would tell him where Izzy had gone.

Now, I'm sitting in the backseat of the car as we head toward the hospital. Gage isn't answering his cell phone, but from what Archer said—he can't. He's completely off grid because of this woman *he's* fallen for. It's crazy to me that my brothers have both fallen in love in the space of a few months - and apparently they both went for broke with their chosen amours.

"We're here." Liam snaps me out of my thoughts as he parks the car.

Climbing out, Liam and I head into the hospital. Several women at the entrance lock eyes on me, and I realize I didn't think this through very well. Truth be told, I wasn't really thinking at all. I'm used to being recognized and swarmed by fans, but I guess I didn't consider that it would happen here. As always, though, Liam is quick on his feet as he escorts me around a group gathering at the entrance.

"Sorry folks—Mr. Winston is here for a personal matter. Give us some room to get inside."

"Fuck. I didn't consider the ramifications of coming through the front entrance." I shake my head as we head toward the front desk. "Excuse me. I'm looking for my brother. His girlfriend, Rhiannon Carmichael, was brought in recently."

"Oh my God." She gasps. "You're Roland Winston from Savage Realm—sir, I'm a huge fan."

Liam leans against the counter. "Ma'am. While he appreciates your enthusiasm, his brother is waiting. Do you mind telling us where he is?"

"Oh. Yes, forgive me." She taps the computer's keys and looks up. "Rhiannon Carmichael is on floor five—intensive care. Take *those* elevators up, but sir, they won't allow you back. It's just for immediate—"

My head swivels toward the bank of silver. "I'm here for him.. Thanks... Kelsey." I smile at her as we hurry toward the elevators. "Intensive care can't be good. I know he said that the Judge tried to kill her—but..."

Liam fills in the blank. "You didn't expect it to be this bad."

Shaking my head as we climb into the box. "No. I didn't. Any luck with Miss Holiday's whereabouts?"

"I've got a few feelers out there, but nothing concrete yet. What I *do* know is she's not *here*. Did she ever mention family to you?"

"She doesn't have any left. Her dad died when we were in high school, and I think her mother recently passed. No siblings." We step out onto the floor, and I pause, scanning the corridor. "Miss." I call out to a nurse who stumbles when she catches sight of me. "Can you tell me which room Ms. Carmichael is in?"

"Um... yes—502. But..."

I smile, making her blush even more. "Thanks, beautiful. Surely it's okay if I just pop in to check on my brother. Who's with her? Come on, Liam."

I don't even wait for her to respond as I trudge past her, scanning the bank of rooms for 502. I can hear faint murmurs coming from inside as we approach the room and I stop to listen. Drake is talking to someone on the other side of Rhiannon.

*"Then I met her. She turned my world upside down in a matter of days. I've broken every rule I had for myself because of her—and I'd do it again if she would just wake up."*

Drake sounds so broken as he speaks. Another voice fills the room as I grasp the handle in my hand.

*"Well, that won't be for a while. The doctors are going to keep her in a drug-induced coma for at least a week. And longer if her scans don't show improvement in her spine. But that's a good thing, Mr. Winston. Plus, looking at her chart, everything else looks good, for her situation at least. Her arm and body will heal, Mr. Winston. But her mind will take longer. Are you prepared to handle all that entails?"*

*"I watched my own father beat my mother so badly she died from the blow to her head. And to make matters worse, my eldest brother had to be the one to end his reign of terror. So yeah… I can handle anything. This woman broke down my walls and I don't intend to walk away—ever."*

I push open the door to find several sets of eyes turning toward me. Seeing my brother look so heartbroken causes me to tear up. Swiping the wetness gathering, I step inside and motion for Liam to follow me.

# 15

# Roland

"Hey. None of that, big brother." I tug him to his feet and wrap him in an embrace.

Like a dam breaking open, Drake sobs against me. "You came."

"Of course, I came. I wish I could have come sooner, but canceling my last show was a bitch."

Drake lets go and steps back. "Canceled your show? Why in the hell did you do that?"

"It's a long story that I won't bore you with right now, and I can't stay long—I've got to get back and try to clear up a misunderstanding between Izzy and me."

"Izzy?" Drake rubs his forehead and closes his eyes. "The publicist, right?"

"Yeah. But don't worry about me. Tell me about *her*." I nod toward Rhiannon. "What are they saying?"

Drake moves back to her bedside and sits down, tugging her hand in his.

"I had no idea you were related. I mean, I should have known, but wow…" A woman I don't recognize blushes when I turn our eyes to her. "God, I'm sorry. You're here for your brother and I'm over here fangirling."

"Don't apologize. Roland is used to the girls going ga-ga over him." Drake huffs out a laugh before pressing a kiss to Rhiannon's knuckles. "Rol, this is Lori Conrad. A former client and now Rhiannon's nurse."

I give her my classic boyish grin, causing her to blush even more. "Nice to meet you, though the circumstances suck."

"Yes, they do, and I promise to make sure I'm here every step of the way with your brother and her family. He helped me and now it's my turn to help him. But if you'll excuse me, I'll leave you alone for a bit. Mr. Winston?" She turns toward Drake, her serious expression back in place.

"Hey, I think you can call me Drake now—no more of this Mr. Winston shit." He gives her a halfhearted smile.

"Right. Drake. If you need anything at all, press the call button. I'm here overnight, so it'll be me coming in." She pulls open the door and steps out.

"I'll walk out with you." Liam smiles at her, quickly moving toward the door. "I have some questions about her long-term care that my boss asked me to inquire about."

"Um, sure. Is that alright, Drake?"

I assume Archer has asked him to inquire about it for Alex Whit-mire, Drake's criminal defense attorney, who's building the case against her shitstain husband. "Yes. Whatever he needs, give it to him."

She stammers her response, a pink tinging her cheeks as she glances between the three of us. "Um... right. Yeah. Okay, follow me."

A woman I didn't realize was in the room chuckles. "That was awkward."

"SHIT, I'm sorry. I should have introduced you right away. Roland. Meet Donna Preston. Rhiannon's mother." Drake motions his hand toward the older woman.

"Sorry, we're meeting like this as well." I take her outstretched hand in mine. "I was hoping it was for something grander. Like an engagement party."

Drake snorts at my joke. "It's a little soon for that, brother. She doesn't even know how I feel, and she might not want that once she wakes up. Heath has robbed her of her freedom; I won't do the same."

"You don't look at her like a possession, like he did," her mother says with conviction. "You look at her with love. If she passes that up, I might send her to a mental ward."

"I won't force her. It has to be her decision and hers alone. I refuse to make her feel like she's broken free of one cage to land in another. She needs time to spread her wings and fly."

"Wow." I pull an empty chair beside Drake and sit down. "You really *are* in love with her. The Drake I know *takes* what he wants."

"She's not a thing to take. Rhiannon is a person to want—and I want her unlike anything I've ever had before. It's going to gut me to let her walk away, but I will. She's shown me I was wrong. I *can* love… and it's her I want to give that love to, if she'll have it."

"Why wouldn't she want you?" I reach out and brush my hand over the blanket covering her leg. "You're a man who puts family first—I'm a testament to that."

He glares at me. "You know why."

"That doesn't define you. Are you saying you and she… haven't…?" My eyes shift to her mother, who's watching us intently.

"Please, dear God, tell me you have." She shakes her head. "The one thing she did confide in me was the lack of—you know. In the bedroom. A man like you looks like he can get the job done."

I can't help the laughter that bubbles out of my chest. Drake shakes his head in embarrassment. "We have."

"Once is all it takes for her to know if it's too much or not." I lean back in my seat and sigh.

"It wasn't like that, Rol."

"Interesting." My eyes narrow at him. "You're telling me you had good ole-fashioned sex with a woman and liked it?"

"JESUS, ROLAND." Drake points at her mother. "Think you could lay off this conversation out of respect for both of them?"

She winks as she walks past us. "Actually, I'll go grab some coffee and let you two hash this out. Though I won't deny I am curious as to what kind of kinks you have."

"Fuck *me*." I die laughing again. "I bet your husband loves you."

Rhiannon's mom clicks her tongue at his statement. "If that were true, his sorry ass wouldn't have put us in this position, nor would he be in jail right this minute when our daughter needs him. By the way, thank you for providing your associate as his attorney. Maybe with Mr. Whitmire, Carl will manage to get off lightly."

"Alex is the best criminal defense attorney in the city. He'll probably have your husband labeled as a victim by the time he's done in court. Which… he kind of is." Drake pins her with a serious look.

"Right. I'll see you two in a few." She slips from the room, leaving us in silence.

"Her dad is involved?" I furrow my brows. "That's fucked up, brother."

Drake nods in agreement. "Yeah. It is. He let his daughter marry Heath to save his own hide. Turns out he's tangled up with Alessandro Hugo pretty deep."

"Wait… the same Hugo…Gage is currently hiding from?" My eyes widen at the sound of his name.

"Yep. The one and only. Have you heard from Hugo again?"

I shrug my shoulders, as if hearing from a thug like Hugo is no big deal. "Nah. Liam scared his man off pretty good."

"Speaking of Liam… he chased Rhiannon's nurse outta here pretty fast." Drake glances at the door.

"Can you blame him? She's pretty hot for an older woman." I smirk, knowing full well that Liam was following her out for more than just a few questions.

"Hey, fuck you, buddy. She's not much older than me." Drake punches me in the shoulder, but grows serious again. "They say she's going to be kept in a coma for at least a week—so her neck can heal more."

"I hate that Gage wasn't here to help you. He really fucked up."

Drake blows out a deep sigh. "He has… but hopefully *this* mess will solve his."

Relaxing my frame against the chair, I smile. "We can hope. Now tell me about the woman who has thawed my brother's frozen heart."

"I actually knew of her in college—she was two years younger than me, so we didn't run in the same circles. I ran into her at the ER the night we left your show. She was the patient Gage needed to tend to. I took one look at her, and my chest clenched. I don't know if it's possible, but I think that was the moment I fell in love with her."

"Nothing's impossible, Drake. Sometimes, you meet a woman, and she knocks you completely off balance. You have no idea how to act or what to say, but you know without a doubt she's the one you want. I'm just glad you got a chance to show her what it could be like with someone who really loves her. Don't fuck it up when she wakes up. There's no guarantee of second chances." I'm interrupted by the sound of my phone ringing. "Fuck. I need to take this. I'll be back." Tapping him on the shoulder, I slide my phone out and hurry out of the room.

"Liam."

"Meet me in the car. I got some information, and we need to take a ride."

After letting the nurse know an emergency came up and to let my brother know, I grabbed the elevator. It feels like it takes forever to get to the first floor. Liam is standing by the car when I get outside.

"What did you find out?" I climb into the front seat at the same time he slides into the driver's seat.

. . .

LIAM BACKS out and navigates onto the street. "We're heading over to her job. I think we might find the answers we need from one of her co-workers—rather, her friend who works with her.."

WE WASTE no time navigating the Atlanta streets and pull into Axel. "She's only been gone, twenty-four hours, but maybe Candice Hill will be able to help us out."

EVERYONE'S EYES are on us as we step inside the office. A woman with bleached blonde hair and tits that look like they're about to suffocate her greets us at the desk. "Mr. Winston. I'm Allison—can I help you with anything?"

LIAM CLEARS HIS THROAT. "We need to speak with Candice Hill."

"HUMPH." She rolls her eyes. "Her? Why do you need to speak with Candice? I'm sure I can help you better."

"ALLISON, YOU CAN RETRACT YOUR CLAWS." An older woman appears from one of the hallways. "He doesn't want your fleas." She arches a brown at Allison, who stomps her foot like a child.

"WHATEVER... I don't want Isabella's sloppy seconds, anyway."

. . .

"Don't mind her—she's in heat. I'm Candice." She extends her hand. "What can I do for you two gentlemen?"

"We're hoping you can help us find Isabella Holiday."

A weird expression mars her face, but she hides it quickly. "Isabella has taken a leave of absence."

Liam tilts his head, assessing her words. "Right, we know... but I thought you were friends. She didn't call you before or after she tendered her resignation?"

Candice shoots him a shit-eating grin. "We *are* friends... which means even if she *called* me, I wouldn't betray my friend's trust by divulging her personal business. Now... is there anything else I can help you with? Perhaps another one of your asinine stunts finally caught up with you. If that's the case, I would be happy to do my job and help you."

"My reputation is intact—so no. I don't need your help. What I need is to know where Izzy went."

She laughs — actually fucking laughs at me. "Sorry. No can do. Now—if you two gents will excuse me, I've got work to do."

We watch as she leaves us standing with more questions than we started with. "She knows something." I glance at Liam.

. . .

"YEAH... she does. But that woman is not going to be easy to crack. I'll make some calls and see what I can find out. For now... you're just going to have to wait."

FUNNY THING IS, I've waited all this time for her to barge into my life again—and I didn't even realize it until she left. Isabella Holiday might have run off for now... but when I find her. Things are going to change.

BECAUSE NOW THAT I've gotten a taste of what I never thought I could have... I'm not going to lose it. Isabella Holiday is going to be *mine*.

# 16

# Roland

WHEN LIAM SAID it would take time, I didn't expect a month would pass by. Izzy has managed to hide so damn well, not even Archer has been able to figure out where she's gone. I pay Candice a visit every couple of days, usually with something in hand to bribe her. I smile, thinking about this morning's encounter.

*"This is starting to make me uncomfortable." Candice laughs when I step into her office. "People are starting to wonder if we're having an affair."*

*Setting the coffee down on her desk, I smile. "They know you have better taste than that—plus, you're a little old for me."*

*Candice throws her pen at me. "Wash your mouth out. I was almost starting to feel sorry for you." She gives me a wicked grin before picking up the cappuccino and pressing it to her lips.*

*"Does that mean you're going to tell me where she is?"*

*"Nope." She pops her lips as she sips the drink again. "Are you ever going to accept she's gone? Roland, she didn't want you to find her. You need to move on."*

*"So, you admit she's hiding. Which means you know where she is."*

*Candice stands and moves around me to the door. Placing her hand on the doorknob, she motions to the hallway. "I have work to do, Roland. Have a great day."*

"What has you smilin' so big?"

Rhiannon is curled up on the armchair opposite me. I've been coming over to Drake's place since she was brought home a few weeks ago. Drake rarely leaves her side, but when he has to take care of something, I come chill out with her.

"What do you mean?" I arch a brow at her and smile. "Can't a guy smile for no reason?"

"You're thinking of *her*, aren't you?"

I give my head a nod just as Drake strolls into the room. "Hello, little bird. Have you been a good patient for my brother?"

"You say that as if I'm going to throw a party in your absence. Speaking of which—where *were* you today?" She stands and waves her hand. "Actually... never mind. I'm going to the bedroom to lay down. Roland—thanks for babysitting me."

I watch as she leaves Drake and me alone. "What the hell did you do to her?"

Drake scrubs his hand down his face. "She thinks I'm treating her like glass because I won't touch her."

"Wait... you haven't touched her at all? No kissing? Hugging?"

"No. I want her to be ready... I hold her at night when she's asleep, but that's it."

Shaking my head, I snort. "That's fucked up, Drake. That woman went through hell at the hands of a man who was supposed to love her. Now... a man who claims the same thing isn't touching her? Come on... even you have to see how messed up that is. She probably thinks you're disgusted with her. Go in there and show her what she means to you. I'm going to head out."

"You're full of suggestions, Little Brother. Maybe you should start taking your own. Where's Izzy?"

Spinning back to him, "Seriously? That's a low blow, Drake. I fucked up the *one* good thing in my life that isn't you or Gage. You want to join me in that venture?" Drake stiffens and I see the remorse in his eyes. "Yeah… didn't think so. Call me later."

I step into the waiting elevator and hold his gaze as the doors close. I love my brother, but sometimes he can be arrogant and, well… dumb as shit. Apparently, it runs in the family.

Knowing I can't go in public without Liam, I opt for my own apartment. I can't get into any trouble if I stay inside, and right now my single tracked focus is winning Izzy back—when I find her, that is. After driving around to clear my head, I finally find myself pulling into my parking garage.

I'm just stepping into the lobby of my building when I spot Liam. He looks alarmed, which causes the hairs on my neck to stand on end. "What is it Liam?"

"It's Gage. There's been an incident and we need to go."

"An incident? Is he hurt?" I falter in my steps, causing Liam to grab me. "Why else would you be here instead of calling?"

"Calm down. He's not hurt… but something bad has happened and we're going to meet Alex Whitmire, Archer, and Drake at the hospital."

"Meet them *where?*"

"Alabama. Roland, it's bad. The woman Gage has been hiding out with was kidnapped. She was—she's not good. Plus, the guy guarding her was taken too. He was executed right in front of her."

"Jesus Christ."

After grabbing a bag and stuffing it full of clothes, I meet Liam at his SUV. Climbing in, I'm silent in my thoughts. "You should know that Mrs. Hill will be meeting with Archer to figure out how to spin this mess to the media"

*Fantastic.* The one woman who holds the key to finding the woman I crave more than life itself, and won't tell me where she is, is going to be with us. Being trapped with her right now is the last thing I want.

"Great. Not only is my family coming apart at the seams, now I'll be forced to see the one person who can lead me to Izzy—the same person who is like a safe deposit box with secrets."

"And the one you don't have the key to." Liam sighs. "Don't worry —I was working on a lead until this happened. Once we get things settled, I'll fill you in."

My cell rings and I glance at the screen. "Drake." I press the device to my ear. "Where are you?"

"Loading Rhiannon into the car."

"Wait… should she be traveling?" I glance over at Liam, who just shrugs.

"I am perfectly capable of riding in a fucking car, Roland Winston."

Cringing, which makes Liam snicker beside me, I reply sheepishly, "You didn't tell me I was on speakerphone."

"I would have thought *Loading Rhiannon into the car* was enough clue that you would be on speakerphone."

"You two assholes are going to need me." She shouts through the phone. "We don't know what's happening with Gage or Poppy."

"Poppy? Is that this woman's name? I feel so out of the loop. I'm sorry I haven't been around for you guys."

"Stop." Drake barks into the phone. "You're barely twenty-five and already hit the top 100 billboard four times. You're allowed to have your own life, Rols. Gage and I are big boys who make our own decisions—regardless of consequences. It's a risk we *both* chose to take, though his was substantially riskier. And it would appear maybe he's found his person. But don't you dare, for a minute, think you could have stopped either of us from taking the hard road to get here. Just promise me you'll make an easier go at finding someone to love."

We spend the next twenty minutes of our ride going over the situation Gage has created. Archer's friend and former military buddy, who owns his own security company, placed one of his men as a protection detail on Gage and Poppy. Apparently, Poppy slipped and fell onto a drinking glass she was holding, causing a pretty nasty cut. The decision was made to take her to the hospital, where her guard would pose as her husband. Only somehow, Hugo Alessandro found out and kidnapped them both. Eventually, Archer and his buddy Perez found where they were holding them. Unfortunately, they'd tortured Poppy and executed the guard, Hunter, in front of her.

Gage, my brother who hates firearms, pulled the trigger to end Hugo's life. Now Poppy is in the hospital—and Gage is in prison. The ride to the podunk town Gage and Poppy are currently holed up in takes several hours. It's dark by the time we arrive, but I waste no time getting out of the car.

"Are Drake and Rhiannon here?"

Liam nods. "Yeah. Archer just texted me. There upstairs—the ICU waiting room."

"God—can my family stay out of the hospital after this? I don't want to see the inside of one for a *long* time unless it's because one of them is having a baby."

Liam laughs, though it feels forced, as we head up to the ICU unit. Drake spots me first and is on his feet. His arms are around me before I register what he's doing. "This is fucked up." He steps back and shakes his head. "Poppy was brought in by ambulance two hours ago. Gage was with her until he was taken into custody for Hugo Alessandro's murder. Alex is already at the police department discussing bail. Poppy, on the other hand isn't doing so well. She's severely dehydrated, and the previous injury she'd gone to the hospital for when she was taken is infected. They've taken her to the operating room to debride the wound and stitch her up - fifteen stitches and nine staples to close it. It will heal, but it won't be pretty, I'm afraid. She has several fractured ribs, and worse—a head injury. Apparently she's had others, so they're worried she won't wake up or if she does… not without long-term issues. Gage is going absolutely insane not being here with her. I spoke to him briefly on the phone and promised to stay here with Poppy. I also need to speak with the PR person the agency is sending—and spin this somehow to keep the media cocks at bay."

Like she was conjured from space, Candice Hill walks in. "Mr. Winston. I got here as soon as I could. I'm so sorry to hear about your family's troubles." Her eyes pan to me. "Roland, sorry we're meeting again like this."

Drake pulls Rhiannon against his side, his gaze flicking between us. "You know each other?"

"You could say that. Roland's last PR manager is my friend and co-worker."

"Holy shit. She knows Izzy?" Rhiannon gasps. "Do you know where she is?"

For the first time, Candice Hill is at a loss for words. She flicks her shiny black hair over her shoulder and sighs. "I'm sorry... I can't answer that. Mr. Winston, how can I help with *this* situation?"

Drake gives me a sympathetic look before turning toward Mrs. Hill. "We need to keep this out of the media's eye if at all possible—at least until we get Gage cleared from all charges."

"Sounds like I have my work cut out for me." She blows out a breath. "Ok. I'm going to get checked into the hotel. Perhaps one of you can meet with me in an hour to go over strategy?"

"Archer will meet with you—he has all the details, and I promised my brother I'd stay here with Poppy."

"Fine. I'll speak with him and then we can talk in the morning. The best thing that could happen is we get her transferred to Atlanta—where I'll have the entire firm at my disposal."

"Don't worry. We aren't staying in this backwoods town any longer than required."

Candice nods and turns to face me. "Think you could give me a ride to the hotel? I took a cab from the airport."

Liam shrugs his shoulders at me. "Drake... I'll get her settled. Call me when you know something more. Rhiannon, do you want to come with me or stay here?"

Honestly, I can't decide if being here is bringing up bad memories for her or not, but I want to help however I can. If that means taking care of my brother's girlfriend while he stays here—I will.

"No. I'm fine Roland. Drake needs me right now. You go ahead and get Mrs. Hill settled."

Kissing her on the cheek, I pull my brother into a hug. "Gage will beat this."

"I know."

Mrs. Hill follows me to the elevator and climbs in without speaking. Liam leans against the back corner, not saying a word. He is well aware of the relentless efforts I've made to get this woman to crack, so he knows being trapped in the elevator with her is pure torture.

"I'm sorry about your brother."

Glancing up at her, I nod my thanks. "Just do what you do best, Mrs. Hill. Keep his reputation clean. My family has dealt with enough shit, and they don't need this. All I care about right now is you doing that for Gage and Alex, getting him cleared of all wrongdoings."

I step off the elevator without waiting for her or Liam. Slipping into the car, I stare out the window into the darkness. Why can't my family catch a break? Wasn't our childhood torment enough?

# 17

*Izzy*

IT'S BEEN NEARLY four months since Roland Winston blew back into my life and imploded every best laid plan I had made. Now, I'm hiding out and working remotely—still trying to protect him, though I'm sure *he* doesn't see it that way. On top of that, I have to figure out how to deal with my own issues. Laying on my side, I flick on the TV only to see the Winston family plastered across the screen. Apparently, the eldest Winston is involved in some kind of murder case and is sitting in jail. Candice, my only friend, seems to have spun it well in the news. The official statement is that he's being wrongly accused of something that's clearly self-defense, but the media is running with their own conspiracy theories.

It's played on a loop non-stop for two weeks and I can't help but think about Roland every time it does. I'm stuck between feeling heartbroken and angry. But it's not his fault—at least, not entirely. I knew what I was getting into when I chose not to walk away from the start.

Turning off the television, I peel myself off the couch and amble into the kitchen. Between the dizzy spells and sleeping non-stop— losing weight is the only thing I do these days that seems certain.

It's like a vicious cycle I can't get out of. The doctor I found here in Savannah is worried I'm dealing with depression on top of everything else.

Maybe he's right.

I did lose *everything*, after all. *Again*.

The vibration of my phone across the countertop makes me jump. When I see Candice calling me, I sigh. She really has become the best friend I never knew I needed. "Hey, Candice."

"Izzy." She sighs into the phone. "I don't know how much longer I can keep your whereabouts a secret."

"What?" My voice raises an octave. "You promised, Candice. And I know I've put you in the most unbelievable situation, but I'm not ready to deal with him."

"He's miserable, Iz. Between what's going on with his brother, plus losing you—I'm worried about him. So is his brother, Drake. They all know I'm keeping something from them, but they don't push."

"Roland is just mad he was rejected. He's being a whiny, spoiled star who isn't getting his way. It's just a game to him."

"I think you're wrong. Please Izzy... just give it some thought. He deserves the truth, don't you think? I've gotta run... I've got to meet Drake about Gage's release. He's getting out of prison at the end of the week. All charges were finally dropped. And Izzy...?"

"Yeah?"

"You deserve to be happy."

Disconnecting the call, her words strike too close to the truth, but right now I hurt too much to face him. Seeing him at the club with that woman left me with raw emotions I still don't know how to decipher. I want to hate him… but the truth is, I refuse to admit that what I feel for him is far from hate.

Glancing at the clock, I realize I've got thirty minutes to make it to my appointment. I'm dealing with so much right now. It's a miracle I'm managing on my own. It's times like these that I really miss my mom. She would have known exactly how to handle this situation.

Climbing into the car, I buckle up and back out. Today should be a happy day. Instead, I'm left with dread. The office isn't far from the house, thank God, because I don't know how long I can sit inside a vehicle without passing out. Which is why I'm here today. I need to have several tests done to see why I'm having so many fainting spells. At first, they just thought I had low blood sugar, but the rapid weight loss and excessive sleeping have them concerned. I worry this isn't just a case of being overworked.

The receptionist greets me with an energetic smile. "Morning Miss Holiday. How are you today?"

"Same as always."

"How about we get you to a room?" She waves me through the door and leads me down the hallway. "Here ya go. Dr. Vallara will be in shortly. While you wait, why don't you slip into the gown?"

As soon as the door shuts, I slip off my dress and tug on the flimsy paper gown. I should buy stock in these ridiculous cover-ups as much as I've had them on lately. Just as I plop down on the table, Dr. Vallara walks in.

"Morning, Miss Holiday. How are you feeling today?"

Glancing up, I take in the older man's appearance. He's in his late fifties, but still a looker. He has a calming presence that makes me feel at ease, despite facing this alone. Smiling at him, I shrug. "Same. I had a fainting spell yesterday. It wiped me out, and I slept for hours afterwards."

He nods, looking at me hopefully, but I shake my head as I admit, "It didn't help. I'm still running on empty all the time. No matter how much sleep I get, it's never enough."

"Well… let's get some blood again and see where we're at. Are you up for that?"

Nodding my head in agreement, "Please. I would like to try to have a normal day—or at least one where I don't end up passing out."

I spend the next hour getting poked and prodded. I swear the amount of blood the nurse drew might leave me with just enough to function for the rest of the day. Of course, I think the worst and worry I have some kind of brain tumor, but he assures me he doesn't think it's anything that serious. Since the bloodwork results are going to take a little while, Dr. Vallara says I should go get something to eat and that he'll call me to talk about the results.

I find myself at a local place that's along the river. The view is beautiful, and I opt to sit outside. My mind is filled with all kinds of thoughts—Roland, my health, my parents. I'm so lost in thought I don't notice when a man plops down in the seat beside me.

"How long are you going to hide from him?"

His voice startles me, and I knock over my water. "What the fuck, Liam? Is *he* here?" My eyes widen and dart around the street nervously, as if someone has put out a hit on me and I've been found.

"Relax. He doesn't even know *I'm* here, Isabella. Or that I know you're living in Savannah."

A waitress cleans up the spill and brings me a new glass. I roll my eyes at the flirty tone she uses when taking Liam's drink order, which only makes him laugh.

"You shouldn't be here." I pinch the bridge of my nose. The last thing I need is him snooping into my life right now. "I left for a reason."

"I'd say so… a big reason." Liam arches a brow at me. "You should tell him, Izzy. He has a right to know—he cares about you."

"Roland doesn't care about anyone but himself. And whatever you think you know—mind your business… please.."

Liam takes a sip of his water. "Why are you doing this alone, Izzy? You know damn well Roland would be here beside you every step of the way. That's the kind of man he is—he grew up in a shitty household, which made him go above and beyond for those he cares about. He wouldn't want you facing this alone."

"Doesn't matter—I've been alone for a long time and know how to handle things myself. Roland is a complication I can't deal with right now. He would freak out and would do something stupid to deal with the stress. Like letting a woman whip him." Liam doesn't seem fazed at all by my remark. "You know, don't you? Of course, you do. You've been at his side for what? Six years?"

Liam gives me a pointed look and I nod. "I thought so. Since he left, huh? Then you, of all people, know why I don't want him to know."

"Jesus. Do you hear yourself? You claim to know him, but you're so quick to judge him without knowing the *why* behind what he does. Roland was *abused*, Izzy."

I narrow my eyes at him with a sigh and Liam exhales loudly like he's explaining something to a toddler. "He thinks the pain is what he deserves when he fucks up. That it's somehow *his* fault when things go to shit. That's why he goes there. That's why he let that woman do those things to him. That's why he does all of it. He's hurting… it doesn't take much…and he thought punishment would make him forget—or worse, atone for the sins he thinks he's committed by simply existing."

I gasp at his truth. I had no idea he lived with that guilt. "I didn't know."

"Of course not. No one does. I only know because Roland got shit-faced drunk recently and told me all his deep dark secrets… including the one involving you. That man craves love—but he refuses to see that he's worthy. Until *you*. He might not know his own feelings right now because he's never had them before. But Izzy… Roland is in love with you. Did you know he hasn't gone to the club since he fucked up with you? And let's talk about the guilt he battles for trying to make a mess to keep you in Atlanta. He didn't aim for things to get out-of-hand like that, but it's all in the past now. He's trying to be a better man for you. If he's not at home, he's either with his brother helping take care of Rhiannon or Poppy, or he's in the studio writing. The man has enough material for albums for *years* to come."

Liam pushes back and stands. "I won't tell him you're here—yet. But Izzy…" He shoves the seat under the table. "I won't lie to him anymore, either, or stand by and watch him withdraw into himself much longer. If that means telling him before you do—I will. He has a right to know why you ran and—" he waves his hand through the air. "—what's going on with you."

I watch as Liam gives me his backside and storms away. Something he said filters into my head. *Roland is in love with you,* and as much as I want that to be true, I can't let myself risk the hurt if he's wrong.

Closing my eyes, I push the plate away from me. The conversation with him has caused me to lose what little appetite I had. Staring off into the sky, I close my eyes and beg for a sign. Truthfully, I have no idea what to do. Liam's right. Roland deserves the truth, but fear keeps me from calling him. He can't handle the stress and I can't be the reason he finds himself in a position to give the tabloids more news.

My cell phone cuts off the inside monologue I'm having with myself. Glancing at the screen, I see Dr. Vallara's office calling. Taking a formidable breath, I hit the answer button and press the device to my ear.

"Hello?"

"Miss Holiday, it's Dr. Vallara—I have some answers for you."

"Is it bad? Do I have a brain tumor?"

He chuckles into the phone. "No… it's nothing like that. Here's the deal. All your symptoms are easily explained and are due to…"

I can hear what he's saying, but the reality isn't sinking in. How the hell can this be my life right now? I should have known nothing would be straightforward with me. Not since Roland blew back into my life and literally obliterated all the plans I had laid out. But this… this is the biggest hiccup of all.

"And you're sure?"

"Positive. You'll need to watch your blood sugar, and I need to run a few more tests. Call the office tomorrow and get something scheduled. I'd suggest keeping snacks around in the event you feel a fainting episode coming on. Otherwise, everything looks great. I'll need to see you in four weeks, unless you have issues. Do you have any questions?"

"No. Thank you, doctor."

Shoving the phone into my pocket, I toss some money on the table and mindlessly walk to the water's edge. The dark color of the river reminds me of my feelings—murky. This news is not what I expected. I wander aimlessly back to my car and head home.

I shouldn't deal with this news alone, but calling him means letting him know how I feel.

And that has me more scared than the bomb the doctor just dropped.

That truth is going to change *everything*.

# 18

# Roland

SITTING across from my brother as he discusses the media strategy with Candice is pure torture. Don't get me wrong... I am beyond elated that Gage is getting out of jail tomorrow—but I'm nowhere closer to finding Izzy. Liam left a few days ago to follow up on a lead about her location. Not hearing back from him yet is making me insane. I'm pretty sure Drake is ready to strangle me over this.

I JUST NEED ten minutes with her. Then maybe I can convince her I want to change—that I *am* changing. Sitting with my therapist helped. Izzy was right about one thing... my childhood scarred me more than I realized. My mind drifts back to our recent session.

*"Tell me, Roland. What is it you're afraid of when it comes to getting attached to someone that's not Drake or Gage?" Henry cocks his head and holds my gaze.*

. . .

*Everything about the way he's looking at me makes me feel exposed. Shifting in my seat, I blow out a breath. "I don't know—being left or worse... betrayed. My brothers think that because I was only four, I don't remember much. But the thing is—I do. I remember everything. The screaming, the abuse... the murder—all of it. I still have nightmares... seeing the things my father did to my mom when she didn't do what he wanted. We lived in this great big house, but the money and all the fancy shit didn't matter. Not when our dad was such a monster."*

*"And how does that make you feel now, Roland?"*

*"Like I'm to blame for what he did. He didn't want me—on more than one occasion, he told me so. Then he'd turn to her*

*and beat the shit out of her. It was like he had a twisted moral compass when it came to me because I was four, so she got what he wanted to give me."*

*"Is that why you seek punishment when you've messed up?" I watch as he writes something on his pad of paper. "The thing is Roland... I don't think you go to the club for gratification at all. You go because your father didn't punish you—so this is your penance for your mom."*

*"Maybe... I've never felt worthy of someone's love. Honestly, not even my brothers. They sacrifice so much for me to have a normal life and here I am fucking up more often than not. I don't want to be this man that pushes people away. It's getting lonely."*

*"The good news is you're only twenty-five, Roland. Your whole life is in front of you now. You just need to decide what you want out of it. Are you*

*going to live under this dark cloud and possibly wind up like your father or…"* He takes a deep breath. *"…go after the love that's waiting for you. Because I truly believe this woman ran to avoid heartbreak. And if I had to guess… she's wallowing in it, anyway."* He shifts his legs and sighs. *"You aren't your parents, Roland. You never will be."*

"HEY, ROLS."

DRAKE'S VOICE penetrates my thoughts, and I look up to find three sets of eyes on me. "What?"

"I ASKED you if you were good with what Candice laid out. Gage comes home in a day, and I want to be sure the media focuses on the good he did and not paint him to be a monster."

FLICKING my eyes between him and Candice, I shrug. "Sure. I trust whatever you guys think is right."

"ARE YOU OK?" Drake narrows his eyes on me. "You've been out of sorts more than normal."

"I HAVE a lot on my mind. Look, I'm glad Gage is getting out. Losing him to prison would have gutted me."

"BECAUSE YOU'RE in love with a woman you can't have."

. . .

GRUMBLING, I correct him curtly. "You mean one I can't *find?*"

ARCHER FROWNS as he pipes up, "We'll find her Roland... I promise you that. There's only so many places to hide. She can't run forever."

I LAUGH as my gaze lands on Candice. "Oh, I'll go after her the minute I have the information I need. But she's completely off-radar and my hopes are starting to die right along with my heart."

MY EYES DRIFT to my brother. "There's nothing more that I want than to look at her in the eyes and tell her that I fucked up and beg for her forgiveness. But more importantly—I need to tell her how much I love her."

CANDICE MAKES a noise with her mouth that borders somewhere between shock and disgust. "Wow."

MY HEAD SNAPS back to meet her gaze. "Wow, what?"

HER HEAD TILTS as she seems to really look at me for the first time. "You really love her, don't you?"

"YEAH, I do. And I fucked everything up." I push my fingers through my unruly hair. I know I look like shit. Sleep has evaded me, and my appetite has gone by the wayside. There just doesn't seem to be any point in going through the motions without Izzy.

"For years, I've let the past haunt me and losing Izzy was the wakeup call I needed help. I've spent the last month exorcizing the ghosts possessing me."

CANDICE LETS out a heavy sigh as she raps her nails across the table. "She's going to hate me for this, but I can tell you're sincere, Roland."

"WHAT?" I turn to look at her. "I'm too tired to talk in riddles, Candice."

DRAKE SPEAKS UP, his irritation as evident as my own. "Mrs. Hill. I don't know what you have against Roland, but keeping him from making things right isn't the road to take. He's made mistakes —hell, all of us have. But I'm tired of seeing my brother wither away to a shell of a man. If you know something, for the love of God, tell him."

SHE LOOKS AT HIM, then cuts her eyes to Archer, who has sat silently by listening. "Don't look at me—I'm pretty sure if you don't tell him, Liam will. Because if there is one thing I know, Liam is like a dog with a bone. And he cares deeply for Roland. You bet your ass if you don't finally cave, Liam will find her. Why make him wait?"

CANDICE GROWLS and mumbles something under her breath before finally pinning me with her resting bitch face. "I swear if you fuck up again, this will cost not only you—but I'll lose a friend. Do you understand me, Roland?"

• • •

Shaking my head, I laugh. "Has your conscience finally gotten the better of you?"

"No… not my conscience. More like my heart, because I know she's just as miserable as you are. And if breaking her trust is what it's going to take to make you both see that you're only hurting each other, then I guess I'll take my risks."

"What are you talking about Candice?"

"Isabella. I'm talking about Isabella."

I narrow my eyes, glaring at her. "Izzy? What about her?"

"Did you know she's been squashing rumors about you? I have my hands full enough with your brothers. I haven't touched anything about you - that's all been her. Even in hiding, she's trying to protect you. She might be trying to ignore how she feels, but I suspect it's exactly how you feel, Roland."

"How the hell does this help me, Candice? Now I feel guilty thinking that all this time it was the PR firm dealing with the drama, only to learn it was her? I thought she quit?"

Candice shakes her head no. "She didn't quit." She blows out a breath. "She's in Savannah, Roland. Izzy's in Savannah."

• • •

LIKE THE NUKE dropped on Hiroshima, my ears fill with a rushing sound and all I can hear is the sound of my heart beating. "Savannah?" My voice comes out in barely a whisper. "How… how do you know?" I take a breath, trying to calm the rage starting to boil in my veins. "Tell me, Candice. How is it you know she's in Savannah?"

SHE TURNS to look at my brother. "Please don't fire me over this. I did this for a friend. I need you to understand that this had nothing to do with our business contract or dealings. My boss doesn't even know where she is."

DRAKE DIPS his chin in understanding. "Mrs. Hill… er, Candice. Just tell him what he needs to know."

HEAVING OUT A BREATH, she blurts, "God help me, but when she came to me and told me—well, that's not important. What matters is she's staying at my house in Savannah. It's a family home that was left to me when my mother died. Anyway… she needed to get out of town, and I told her any time she needed it, it was hers. But Roland—you can't just bust down her door. There are things you don't know, and I can't tell you." She pins me with a sorrowful gaze. "Just know that she didn't leave without a good reason. At least a reason she thought was good enough."

"FUCK THAT." I push back, knocking over my chair. "Tell me where. Give me the address or so help me God I'll—" My words come out like venom.

· · ·

"OR YOU'LL WHAT?" Candice stands, getting in my face. "I'm the one with all the cards here, Roland. You don't know the address, so stop fucking threatening me. Jesus."

"ROLAND." Archer interrupts. "No need to threaten Mrs. Hill. Here—" he slides a piece of paper across the surface of the table. "The address." He smirks at Candice, who simply rolls her eyes.

"NOW YOU DON'T HAVE to worry about being called out by Izzy for betraying her. You didn't give me the address, Archer did." Turning to ask Drake if I can leave, he simply shakes his head at me.

"YOU DON'T NEED my approval, brother." He tosses me his car keys. "Go after her. Get your woman and bring her back home."

I START toward the door and pause. Glancing over my shoulder, "Candice?" She arches a brow at me. "Thank you. I promise not to fuck this up. She won't be pushing me away this time."

AS I START TO LEAVE, she calls out to me again. "Roland—wait." I pause, shooting her a quick look. "When you get there— remember that she left because she thought she was protecting you."

"CANDICE, there isn't anything she could tell me that would make me run. I let her walk away two times in my life—the first we were just kids. The second time was because I was a fool. It won't happen a third time."

.  .  .

"Just remember that Roland. Because even the best of us aren't prepared for some truths."

I don't speak to anyone as I rush from Drake's office and hitch a ride on the elevator down to the parking garage. Slipping in behind the wheel of his car, I punch in the address. It's almost four hours from here, and the ride is going to feel longer than eternity. Hurrying to my penthouse first, I barely register that I've made it in my place and packed before I'm back on the road. I could switch cars, but Drake is already gassed up, saving me time. Glancing at the clock on the dashboard, I note it'll be close to nine at night when I finally arrive.

For shits and giggles, I pull up her number and hit call. I don't expect her to answer since she's sent every other call from me straight to voicemail, but I have to try. When the familiar greeting fills the interior of my SUV, I'm not at all surprised. But this time I don't hang up... this time I wait for the beep to let me know I can speak.

As soon as the piercing sound bounces off the interior, I take a deep breath and let the words I've bottled up come out.

"Izzy... I don't know what's happening right now—but I know this. I fucked up. I hurt you in ways I didn't mean to. And worse, I hurt myself. You've done a good job staying under the radar, Freckles... but hide and seek is about to end. You can run, Izzy. But I'll find you. And when I do–I'm not letting you go again."

. . .

I DISCONNECT TO CALL LIAM. "Hey Rols. I should be home in a day. I'm hoping—"

I CUT HIM OFF. "Stop. Liam, I know where she is. I'm headed to Savannah."

"FUCK. Well, then I should tell you that's where I am. I found her and went to see her, but it didn't go like I planned. Which is why I was waiting to tell you."

"IT'S OKAY. I'm going to have to force her to talk to me. Candice said she left to protect me and, from what, I have no idea. But I'm coming and she can't run anymore."

LIAM'S SIGH comes through the speaker loud and clear. "Maybe you should come to my hotel first. I think I should fill you in on what I've learned."

"NO. I want her to tell me herself why she ran. Liam, I love her and there is nothing that will make me leave her again."

"I HOPE you're sure about that, Roland. Because some things are bigger than you're ready for."

Grunting as I change lanes to stay on I-75 south, I snarl, "Why does everyone keep saying that? What is it that you think will make me leave? No–you know what? Don't tell me, Liam. Because I won't run like her. Not now—not ever. I'll call you when I get to Savannah, but I'm going straight to her."

"Fine. I'll give you time with her, but when you're ready, call me. We can figure out how to proceed." Disconnecting, I settle into my seat and concentrate on driving.

Hang on, Izzy. Because ready or not... Here I come.

# 19

*Izzy*

TODAY WAS the worst day I've had since arriving here in Savannah. After passing out at the park and then backing into a firetruck two hours later, I am ready to crawl in a hole and die. Not literally—but seriously, can this day get any worse?

Fixing myself something to eat, I pad my way into the living room and plop down on the overstuffed cushions. Grabbing the remote, I flick through the channels until I land on Fifty Shades Darker. Immediately, my mind drifts to Roland, making my heart squeeze inside my chest. Maybe Dalton was right when he said this movie made the idea of living an alternative lifestyle taboo. I watch the characters on screen try to navigate finding a middle ground in their vastly different needs and wonder if that could have been me and Roland—if I hadn't run.

I'll never know, not anytime soon, anyway. Shoving my bowl to the coffee table, I snuggle into the heap of blankets I've piled on the sofa and let the warmth drag me into a semiconscious state. I'm tired, but no matter what I do, falling asleep seems to be like finding a diamond in the rough. Giving up on trying to catch some shuteye, I decide I'm well overdue for some self-care.

I haul myself up from the nest I've created on the couch and climb the stairs. A nice, long, hot shower is just what I need to wash away this utterly bizarre day. After flicking on the water, I strip off my leggings and t-shirt. The changes I've faced since coming to Savannah are monumental, and I'd be lying if I said they didn't frighten me. Having no one to call except Candice, I feel completely alone.

The hot water prickles against my skin as I climb beneath the spray. Candice minced her words when she told me about this condo. Apparently, it belonged to her great-grandmother and has been passed down from her grandmother to her mother—and now her. It's absolutely gorgeous and I could see living in something like this, but that's just a pipe dream. Eventually, I'll have to go back to work, but what client is going to hire me in this state?

Finally, turning off the water, I step out and wrap a towel around my body and don one on my head. Bracing myself against the sink. I scrub my palm across the fog-covered mirror and sigh. My eyes have lost their luster and my skin, while normally pale, has a sallow appearance. Coupled with the massive amount of weight loss, I look like a walking caricature of my former self, like a specter hanging around to haunt those who did me wrong. Only, I'm still breathing... for now.

Needing something other than this wallow of self-pity I'm in, I tear off the towel and run it through my auburn red locks. Kicking on the blow dryer, I fan it across my hair. The sound of the dryer gives me a strange sense of peace and I drift to thoughts that do me no good.

Two days ago, I dealt with a couple of old photos that resurfaced on the internet. Roland's muscled body was splashed across several online trashy news outlets, so I spent hours issuing cease and desist letters—not to mention threatening lawsuits if they continued to use photos that had been obtained illegally. Of course, no one wants to admit to publishing them and I haven't been able to figure out where the hell they came from. I guess that's a moot point since they're gone again. If only the label would see it from my point of view.

Seeing him like that only stirs emotions I refuse to deal with. After finishing my hair, I tug on some leggings and an oversized shirt. Looking down at the cotton fabric, I shake my head. It's Roland's—one that managed to wind up at my apartment. Why I took it, I don't know.

That's a stone-faced lie. I know exactly why I took it. As much as I want to forget him—I can't. The bastard has my heart and doesn't even realize it. It's just a little after eight at night, and I have nothing to eat in the house. At least nothing that sounds like it'd stay down, so I head out to the grocery store in hopes of finding something to sustain me another night.

I was going to go by after my visit to the park, but my episode left me exhausted, so I came home. But now I'm hangry. And according to the doctor, I need to eat even when I don't feel like it. Which reminds me, I need to pick up more testing lancets. Finding out my blood sugar is fucked up, on top of everything else, was just another kick to the gut.

Careful to park in a manner that will prevent any more fender benders, I climb from the car and head inside. There are hardly any people inside, making me happy. Dealing with people is the last thing on my mind. As I pace the aisles, I can't help overhearing a young woman on the phone.

"Can you believe they postponed the concert? Yeah... only two more months, thank God. I love Savage Realm."

My heart drops at the mention of Roland's band. "Excuse me." I interrupt her, causing her to give me a snarky look.

"Um... what?" She raises an eyebrow. "Hold on, Amber. Someone needs to ask me something. I dunno—maybe she hit my car or something." She lowers the phone. "What, Lady? You hit my car or something?"

"What?" I shake my head. "No... I didn't hit your damn car. I heard you talking about Savage Realm. Did you say they postponed the concert?"

"*You* like them? Wow—I wouldn't take you for a fan." Rolling my eyes, I wait for her to answer my question. "Any who... yeah, they postponed the one in Austin. I bought plane tickets and everything to go—it pisses me off."

"Maybe they had a good reason. I'm sure you can get your tickets changed."

I spin on my heel and rush to the register. I'm still pissed he's taking risks with his career like that.. As I slide into my car, a wave of dizziness hits me, and I drop my head to the steering wheel. It hits me that he probably postponed it because of his brother, making me feel guilty for acting like a bitch. His behavior only confirms my suspicion that the real Roland is buried under years of pain.

The dizzy spell finally passes and I slowly back out—careful to watch for fire trucks. Rounding the corner to the house, I'm surprised to see my neighbor's house lit up. Mrs. Croone's an older woman who doesn't usually leave everything on like that, but I notice a car I don't recognize parked on the curb in front of her house. Parking in the drive, I gather my bags and start toward the front door. As I near the front stoop, I spot something at the base of the door. Setting down the groceries in my hand, I squat.

"What the fuck?" I mutter into the evening sky.

A black leather cuff stares at me from the cement porch. A leather cuff that is all too familiar to me. Grabbing the band in my hand, I push to my feet and look around. There's no way this is coincidental. This tiny object means the one person I've been hiding from was here.

Pushing the worn bracelet against my nose, I inhale, and the familiar woodsy scent assaults my nose, bringing tears to my eyes. Clutching it to my chest, a sob rips from me as I scan the yard. I snap the cuff on my wrist and unlock the door. Mrs. Croone might have seen him, so I hurry to put up my things and go next door.

My knuckles barely hit the wooden door before she's pulling it open. "Oh, dear… I was worried about you, Isabella. I thought that crazy man had done something to you."

"Crazy man?" I clench my fists, following her inside. "What are you talking about? I was at the store…. Mrs. Croone, was someone at my house?"

"Yes, dear. Some man in a leather jacket was making a racket at your house. He wouldn't stop banging on the door and when I told him he needed to go, he told me to fuck off. Can you believe that? Anyway, I called the cops on him. I watched as he told them he wasn't leaving your house. He didn't look thrilled to be carried off in handcuffs—but you know this police department doesn't play."

My heart beats uncontrollably, and I feel my head spinning. Bracing myself on the table, I take a steadying breath. "Mrs. Croone, was the man at my door tall with blonde hair?"

"Yes. Oh, my goodness… has he been harassing you?"

Shaking my head, I fight the urge to pass out. "No… nothing like that. He's a—friend."

"Oh. Dear, are you alright?" She pulls out a chair, waving me into it. "You look rather pale. I'm sorry if I screwed up. I just know you're a single gal and seeing him so crazed like that—I feared he was here to do you harm."

If she only knew how close to the truth she is. Roland *will* do me harm, but not in the manner she thinks. My head spins and as I glance up to meet her eyes, I know I'm about to lose the battle for the second time today.

"I'm not feeling well… I think I might go home."

Standing, I wobble on my feet. "Maybe you should just wait a second. You don't look well, Isabella."

"I'm fi—"

And just like that, the shitty day becomes one for the record books as I pass out and hit the floor like a sack of potatoes. I vaguely hear Mrs. Croone as she speaks to me, but the dizziness wins, and I give in to the darkness. The last thing that flashes through my mind is—Roland is *here*.

20

# *Roland*

THIS IS NOT how I wanted to start my attempt to win Izzy back. Sitting in this dank jail cell has my insides twisted up and my anger bubbling at an atomic level. When I found Izzy's house, I wasn't expecting to encounter a nosy fucking neighbor.

Sure, I definitely made a scene and wouldn't leave until Izzy answered the door and told me to take a hike—but I didn't expect the old bat to call the cops. That was unexpected. And now I'm sitting here until Alex can get down here and post my fucking bail.

Today's the day Gage gets out of jail… and the irony is not lost on me because now I'm the one needing bail money. The worst part, I'm not even there to welcome him home. If Izzy was in my arms, I wouldn't feel so damn guilty. I've never been in jail, so this is the first and, hopefully, last time I'll ever have this experience.

"You look restless over there, pretty boy."

My cellmate's voice has me sitting up from the bench and stretching. "Irritated is more like it."

The older man was brought in drunker than Cooter Brown. He smelled like an entire bottle of Whiskey had been dumped on him, and looking at him this morning, you wouldn't even know it. "What'd ya do to get in here? You don't look like a hardened criminal." He chuckles at his own joke.

"Disorderly conduct and resisting arrest."

He purses his lips as if he's thinking. "Hum. You got someone to get you out?"

Nodding yes, I reply, "Yep. They should be here any time now."

The older man's expression is vague as he sighs, "Not me this time. My daughter is done with me. I ain't been right since her ma died. The bottle became my stand-in lover. You ever been in love, boy?"

My mind immediately goes to Izzy. "Not until recently. That's what I'm doing here. Trying to win her back—and this isn't going to help. What's your name?"

"Max Winder. What about you—does anyone ever tell you that you look like that guy from Savage Realm?"

"Yeah, a time or two. I'm Daniel." I give him my middle, hoping to keep this fuckup out of the media and keep the ruse up—this is the first time someone hasn't recognized me and I kind of like it.

He rubs his chin. "You could be the subdued version of him."

Snorting at his statement that I'm not hype enough to be me, I reply,. "Right... because he's definitely more put together." I hold my hand out to him. "I might need a career change after this, if this arrest gets me fired."

"Over disorderly conduct and resisting arrest?" Nah. Unless you work for the CIA or something, I'm sure others have been arrested for far worse than that. Your lady knows you're in here?"

"She doesn't even know I'm in Savannah." I can't believe the turn of events in the last twenty-four hours. I finally figure out where she is, and I fuck it up by getting arrested. "We had a falling out over something I did, and she left town. It's taken me weeks to find out she was here the whole time."

"If it's the real deal, fight for it. Don't be an old drunk like me who loses everything over his misguided belief his life isn't worth anyone or anything but a bottle."

"You said you have a daughter?"

"Yeah. She's married with kids. After the last time she had to bail me out, she told me to lose her number. Addy, that's her name, reminds me so much of her mother and now, I don't even have *her*. Can't say I blame her—I wouldn't want me around kids either."

I watch the old man closely. "Why don't you get sober? Start fresh and spend the time you can with your family? I'd give anything to have a normal family."

"It's too late and I'm too broke to get the help I really need. You don't have a family?" He tilts his head at me in confusion. "Your parents, they not around anymore?"

Not wanting to divulge the dirty Winston secrets, I smile. "Something like that."

"Pretty Boy." The guard shouts from the other side of the bars, causing me to jerk. "Let's go—your bail has been posted."

"Looks like you're getting outta this joint." Max holds his hand out again. "Go get her, boy. Don't let go when you do. Time is short— so make it count."

Gripping his hand in a firm handshake. "You do the same, Max."

The officer leads me down the hall and through a set of double doors. Both Liam and Alex are standing at the counter, and I don't miss the ragey look Liam is giving me. "What the fuck, Roland? Why didn't you call *me* last night? I could've had you out of here then."

"I needed Alex to work his magic and get these trumped-up charges dropped." I sign some paperwork and grab my wallet. Noticing my bracelet is not with my personal items, I look up at the officer. "Was there a leather cuff with my things? It's not here."

He rifles around, "Nope. That's everything."

"Fuck." My fingers instantly go to my wrist. Turning toward Liam and Alex, "Let's go. I still need to talk to Izzy."

We make it to the front door, and I pause. My thoughts stray to the old man I shared my cell with. I felt the heartache he was harboring as he talked about his wife and daughter. I know without a doubt if Izzy tells me to get lost, I'll be just like Max—lost. Spinning on my heel, I march back up to the counter. "How much is Max Winder's bail?"

"That old drunk?" The officer keys in something on the computer. "$2,500. You know this is a regular occurrence for him—he'll just be back tomorrow night if he gets out."

Alex steps up beside me. "What the hell are you doing, Roland?"

"Sometimes people just need a push. Give me your checkbook, Alex. I know you still carry one around." My eyebrow arches, daring him to tell me otherwise.

He tugs it out of his jacket pocket and hands it over. "Of course, I do… at the rate you and your brothers are going, I can't leave home without it. And it's not mine—it's the company's."

I scribble out the amount needed and rip it from the leather case. "Here. Do you have an envelope and paper I can write on?"

"Do I *look* like a secretary?" The smug cop smirks.

"How about front row tickets to my concert? Or is that considered paying off a government official? On second thought—how about you be a decent fucking human and help me out?"

He rips off a piece of yellow legal paper from a nearby pad and hands it to me. "That's the best I can do."

Rolling my eyes, I hurriedly write my message to Max. I wasn't kidding when I said sometimes people need a push in the right direction. And even though I'm sure his daughter has begged him to get sober, it's probably not enough. "Can you get this to him?" I hand over the canary-colored paper. "Seriously—it's important you don't lose that. Max needs it."

"Yeah. Whatever. He'll be processed out next since you're an idiot and paid his bail."

Handing over Alex's leather book, I shrug. "I've been called worse. I'd say thanks for the stay, but the accommodations could use some work - and the hospitality ain't shit, either."

We head out of the police station and climb into Liam's car. "Where to?" He grumbles, still pissed I didn't call him.

"How long you going to pretend to stay pissed at me? I told you why I called Alex and not you. Besides, sitting in the cell gave me time to think."

Alex chuffs a laugh, "You couldn't have gone to a park or a library to do that? Jesus, you Winston boys are going to make me gray-headed before my time."

"Hate to break it to you, Alex—you're already gray." Liam cracks the joke as he pulls off the curb. "Did you even talk to Izzy last night before winding up in the tank, Rols?"

"No… as it turns out, she wasn't home. I thought maybe she was just ignoring me, which is why I was being so loud." Liam pulls up to the curb outside Izzy's house and parks. "I had no idea she was living next to a cranky ass old woman."

"Well, how about this time we don't make a big scene?" Alex and Liam climb out and I realize I'm going to get to do this with an audience. "At least, not at first—it might be unavoidable when you tell her it was you who leaked the pictures this last time in a desperate attempt to get her back. I still can't believe your dumb ass thought that would work. You better be glad Candice was able to work magic and get them taken down... *again.*"

"Whatever Alex. I know it was Izzy who got them struck from the web since she never actually quit, which means it was actually a *brilliant* idea."

Alex nudges me and smirks. "Well, it didn't exactly work out like you hoped, did it?"

I glare at him, "It could have, if Candice wasn't covering for her... or you know, Liam keeping things from me."

Liam holds up a hand in defense. "Trying to figure out how to tell you without setting off a ticking time bomb is not keeping things from you. And I was obviously right, since you about lost your damn mind last night."

I cross my arms and give them both a knowing look. "You don't understand what it's like to be in love and lose it. If you were in my shoes, you would have done the same damn thing." I start up the sidewalk and pause, nearly making the two of them collide into me. "You can stay in the car. I don't need babysitters."

"Your arrest last night begs to differ. We'll leave you two alone once we know she isn't going to call the cops - or clock you."

I've barely made it up the steps when I hear the old biddy next door. "You–hoo!" She's waving her arms frantically. "Izzy's friend!"

"Great… someone let her outside." I grumble, turning my attention toward the woman. "Ma'am, I promise not to make a scene this time—but I need to talk with Izzy."

"I know." She waddles down her steps and shuffles through the connected yards. "But she isn't home. Gosh, I feel so terrible about last night. I had no idea you two were friends…Roland, right? I thought you were some kind of crazy person, you see. I didn't mean to upset her—she's not well, you know."

The hairs on my neck stand on end. "What do you mean, she's not well?" I glance back at the closed door to Izzy's place and wonder if she's inside—sick.

"I don't know… she's really private. But last night when she got home, I told her what happened—and well…" She twists her hands in front of her and I notice her eyes are filling with tears.

"Hey… I'm not mad at you." I step down off the concrete porch and press my hand to her shoulder. "I kinda deserved it. But you said you told her last night—is she inside?"

"No." She clears her throat. "I didn't know she'd react the way she did… I promise. If I had known she was ill, I would have made her stay sitting. But Izzy's kind of stubborn and when I told her about your visit—she passed out."

"*Passed out?*" I stiffen. "Is she home alone now? Jesus Christ." Alex moves out of my way as I start up the steps.

"Wait… she's not there. When I couldn't wake her, I called 911. Roland, Izzy is at Memorial Hospital."

The blood rushing to my ears is all I hear. It isn't until Liam's hands are on my shoulders, guiding me to the car that I hear him speak. "Thank you ma'am. We'll take him there now. Come on, Rols, get in the car."

"What the hell is wrong with her?" I look over at Liam. "I should have been here for her. She shouldn't be sitting in a hospital alone."

Liam's lips press into a thin line. "You know something—you tried to tell me on the phone. Jesus Christ, Liam… is it bad?"

"Just talk to her, Roland. And listen to everything she has to say. I believe Izzy loves you and this—" he waves his hand in the air as if calling out her move to Savannah, "…was her way of protecting you."

"We're here." Alex presses his hand against my shoulder. "Let's go find out where she is."

The inside of the ER is bustling with a ton of people, but I don't care and push through to the front desk. I can hear murmurs of my recognition, but I block them out. "Excuse me." I squeeze my eyes shut. This is all too familiar again. "Can you tell me where Isabella Holiday is? She was brought in by ambulance last night."

"Are you family?"

Liam steps forward, "He's her fiancé."

"She hasn't marked the privacy indicator on her check-in, so I guess I can tell you. Miss Holiday was moved into a temporary room— 302 until they can move her upstairs."

I don't wait, and beeline for the elevator. Liam is standing beside me as we climb inside the metal box. "Alex is going to go grab some coffee and meet us up there. He's also calling your brothers to let them know what's going on."

Tightening my fingers into a fist against my leg, I sigh. "I can't lose her, Liam. What if—" I swipe my hand down my face, trying to quell the tears. "What if I'm destined to be alone?"

"You're not, Roland. Make her talk to you, ok?"

We step off the elevator and find her room immediately. The door is closed, and I take a deep breath and turn to Liam. "It's not like she can go anywhere—do me a favor and make sure I get at least ten minutes before she has me thrown out. That's all I need."

"Deal."

21

*Izzy*

THE STEADY BEEPING sound penetrates my sleep and I slowly come awake. My head feels like a rhino stomped all over it and I wince as the fluorescent lights burn into my retinas. It takes a second to get my bearings, but it doesn't take a genius to realize I'm in the hospital. Flashes of Mrs. Croone wash over me, and I remember everything from the night before. Finding Roland's bracelet, her saying he got arrested, everything...

Thoughts of Roland make me tense, wincing at the tug of the IV strapped to my arm. "Hey... you're awake."

Like the devil himself has been conjured, Roland's gruff voice washes over me. Turning my head slightly, I realize he's here—sitting beside me and holding my hand. I stare down at our connected palms and blink. His thumb brushes across the tops of my knuckles and I can't seem to tear my eyes away from the movement. Him being here creates a wealth of confusion—both for his presence and the butterflies that seem to have suddenly migrated to my belly.

"Freckles?" He calls me by the nickname I long to hear from his lips. Glancing up, I find his eyes are zeroed in on the cuff wrapped around my wrist. "You're in the hospital, Izzy. You passed out and wouldn't wake up. You've been here since last night."

"How are you here?" I find my voice, though it sounds foreign to me–like someone else has spoken. "I... I thought you were in jail."

Roland tilts his head, the look marring his face one I haven't seen in a long time, and it's one that makes my heart kick up a notch. "Izzy... I got out this morning, but me being in jail is a minor nuisance. But *you* laying here in this bed is—*Fuck, why didn't you tell me?.*" He rubs his face with his free hand. "This is more important than any of that other bullshit."

Looking at him more closely, I can see the strain of the last few months in his eyes. His hair is disheveled, and he has a few days of facial hair dusting his skin. Not to mention the shine in his eyes seems to be dulled—he looks *tired*. I'm to blame for some of this. Running like a coward, I left him with a broken heart. Seems like my leaving solved nothing, and now an even bigger problem lies between us. I start to speak, ready to confess everything, but Roland sighs and starts talking before I can.

"I never thought anything could top the way I felt seeing my dad torture my mom in front of me. Not even the night my mom died, and Gage killed my dad—did I feel like *this*. Of course, I was terrified—that my brother, the one I looked up to, was going to die with him. And then they hauled him out of the house in handcuffs. I remember not being able to breathe. For years, I've been chasing pain to avoid not knowing when it would come because my entire childhood was filled with nothing but agony. I watched my dad rape and beat my mother so many times, I can't even count them all. Not to mention the times he told me I was nothing to him—he hated me, hated my very existence. Sure, my aunt was loving and kind when she took us in, but the damage was done. It's still hard to believe a woman as sweet as her was related to the vile thing that created me. Julie made sure I got counseling and tried to show me what love really looked like. But it was just too late. I couldn't let go of the poison he'd filled me with."

"I've done some stupid shit, Freckles, but the night I called you to the club, those feelings from when I was a kid rose to the surface. My reasons were stupid for going there. I needed something to erase the feelings I got when I heard them talking about you leaving. Otherwise, I was going to explode with helplessness. I didn't know it then, but what I was feeling was—no, *is* love. That's an emotion I can't express or put into words because I've never felt it. Don't get me wrong, I love my brothers. They're all I have in this world... well, *were* all I had."

He brushes his thumb across my hand, the movement slight but filled with a thousand meanings. "Even when you disappeared, the pain of losing you wasn't something I could escape. But nothing..." He glances up at me. "Nothing can compare to how I felt walking into this room last night. Seeing you laying here, looking so fucking frail—damn, Izzy. I think my heart stopped."

"Roland." His name comes out as a whisper. I don't even know how to process his admission. It's more than I've ever gotten out of him, and it's filled with so much emotion, I can't even digest it. I've waited forever to hear this man say he loves me, and now that he has, I'm scared shitless. The truth I've kept from him might be the thing that takes away the one thing I want—him. "I don't know what to say, But I'm sorry. I'm sorry I didn't tell you sooner."

"You don't have to say anything, Freckles." His voice cuts me off as he stands from his chair and settles himself on the edge of my bed. The feel of his palm against my cheek cracks open the dam, holding back the tears. "Don't cry. Please... I can't stand to see your tears. I've caused enough of those to last a decade. I came here to tell you I can't live without you, Izzy. This is not how I planned to share my deepest, darkest secrets with you—but it is what it is. If you'll have me, scars and all, I want to try again." His thumb swipes away a teardrop. "Freckles, talk to me. The truth this time… are you sick? How bad is it?"

My heart thunders against my ribs because I realize he *doesn't* know. Those words aren't because he feels guilty… they're just him grasping at straws. This is the moment I should tell him why I ran. Until now, I couldn't see Roland handling things well. He still may not—but now I see I should have trusted him enough to give him the chance. The guilt I feel threatens to pull me down, and as I open my mouth to tell him, a sob slips past my lips instead. Roland tightens his hold against my palm, but as he leans in to press his lips against mine, the door opens, and we're interrupted by Dr. Vallara.

"Glad to see you're finally awake, Miss Holiday." He glances at Roland, who jerks back and sits tall on the mattress like the doctor didn't just interrupt something intimate. "I'd like to talk with you about the results of the newest tests I've run."

I flick my eyes to Roland and swallow. "Dr. Vallara, this is Roland Winston. He just got here, and I haven't had a chance to catch him up on…" I clear my throat and sigh heavily as I admit, "…anything."

He gives me a comforting smile. "Perhaps he could step out then? I don't think this is how he wants to find out."

Roland tenses and squeezes my hand. "Izzy. Whatever is going on, I'll be right here. There isn't anything he could say that's going to make me run away from you again." He holds my gaze as he pulls my hand to his lips and places a kiss across my knuckles. "Let me be here for you."

This has 'train wreck' written all over it, but for whatever reason, the thought of him leaving me alone is far worse. Swallowing my nerves, I nod. "You can stay, but know this isn't how I wanted you to find out, Roland. I planned to tell you when I was ready to face you—but not like this."

"It's fine, Freckles. We can handle this together."

Closing my eyes, I send a prayer up to the heavens that this doesn't blow up like a bomb detonating. When I open them again, both men are waiting for me to speak. "It's fine, doctor. You can speak with him here—he was going to find out sooner or later, anyway."

"Right." He clears his throat. "Well, your blood work shows your sugars are finally normal and your blood pressure is where I expect it to be for someone in your condition." I glance at Roland to see if the words are registering, but he is watching the doctor speak with rapt attention. "You've lost a few more pounds than I like, but we can manage that with diet changes. Then there's your iron—it's low, so we'll start you on some different supplements—which I've already started." He points to the bag hanging on her left side. "But your food intake has to get better."

Roland glances down at me, and then back to the doctor. "What's going on, Freckles? Do you have cancer—is that why this is happening to you? Doc," he cuts his gaze to him. "What are her treatment options?"

Dr. Vallara blinks in confusion, "Um... Mr. Winston—Miss Holiday doesn't have cancer."

"She doesn't?"

"No." He glances at me, uncertainty filling his eyes. "Miss Holiday?"

Roland looks at me, his eyes filled with such fear, it nearly guts me. I can see the remnants of a scared little boy burning in the pools of blue, and I hate myself for letting him become that person. "I wanted to tell you—so many times I picked up the phone to call you, but I was scared." Tears roll down my face as I continue. "I don't think I ever really stopped loving you, Roland. And knowing I can't be the woman you need, I knew I needed to walk away—but then this happened. Please know that I didn't do this on purpose. And I don't blame you either. At first, I was mad… but then I realized even if I couldn't have you," I grip his hand in mine. "I'd have a part of you forever." He furrows his brows in confusion. "I don't want this to be the reason you stay, Roland. I planned to deal with it alone—and figure it out. And maybe that's wrong on my part, but I didn't want to burden you while you were trying to get your career in order. I'm sorry—truly, I am."

"Just fucking tell me… because I' not following you Izzy. I just told you I love you. I meant every fucking word, and it's not because I feel like I owe you something." He tugs my hand against his chest. "You feel that? My heart is beating for you, Freckles. No matter what, you or he—" Roland points to the doctor. "—says. I'm not going anywhere."

Taking a deep breath, I summon the strength from somewhere deep inside me. Roland looks at me with such passion, I don't doubt his words for a second. I truly believe he loves me—and God, I love him. Every fucked-up road has led us back to each other and I pray to all the supreme beings out there to let me have this one thing… let him stay even after I tell him what's burning on my tongue.

"Roland… I'm not sick—" The doctor clears his throat as he gives me a look and I concede, "…okay, I *am*, but… not like you're thinking." He waits, holding my gaze as I take a deep breath and spill the life-altering words. "I'm pregnant, Roland."

## 22

### Roland

MY BRAIN HEARS HER WORDS, but it doesn't absorb them. I can kinda hear her saying my name, but I can't tear my eyes off the leather bracelet she's wearing—*my* leather bracelet. Izzy is donning the cuff I've had since making it big with the Savage Realm. I've never taken it off and seeing her wearing it does something to my insides. I slump into the seat beside her bed, letting the atomic bomb she just dropped marinate inside me.

"You're wearing my bracelet." The words spill out, as dumb as they are, and then the realization of what she *said* hits me. "And you're having *my* baby."

I lift my head to find her face wet with tears. The room is empty now, leaving us alone with this momentous news. Izzy picks up on my glances toward the door and sighs. "I sent him out. I figured we needed a moment alone—since I just dropped some kinda big news on you."

"You're pregnant."

She smiles, though it doesn't reach her eyes. "Yeah, Roland. I'm pregnant."

"And it's making you sick." I straighten my back as my eyes fall closed. "See... even my spawn is poisonous." Grunting, I attempt to tug my hand out of hers, but she holds me tight, halting the motion. "Izzy... I've literally trapped you with something you'll never be able to escape."

"Roland." She fights back tears, her voice cracking. "Your *baby* isn't what's making me sick. It's the fact that I'm not eating—you heard the doctor. My body isn't adjusting to your overachieving sperm because I'm not getting nutrients. And don't you dare say this baby is poison... it isn't."

My gaze snaps back to hers. "You're having a baby... my baby is in your stomach right now." My eyes trail down her frame and stop at her lower half. I hadn't noticed it before, but there's a slight swell to her abdomen. Instinctively, I reach out and press my hand over the tiny bump. "You're having my *baby*."

"We've established that, Roland. I'm pregnant—with *your* spawn," She deadpans as she says the word. She's trying to seem mad about it, but even under the monosyllabic response, I see her eyes light up.

"Fuck." I grunt, dropping my head to the mattress. "I'm not prepared to be a father, let alone this soon. I don't even have a *clue* what it takes to raise a baby..."

Her fingers push through my hair, and I breathe out at her touch. "I don't expect anything from you, Roland. I know your life isn't built for a baby, but I didn't exactly plan to have you around, so I'm prepared...mostly..."

Turning my head, I lay my cheek against her side, her words threatening to rip me open. "Music isn't as important as you are, Freckles. Without you, I can't write a damn thing, nor do I want to."

I sit up and slide back onto the edge of the bed. Cupping her face with my hands, I hold her gaze. The deep green orbs are tainted with emotion—emotion I helped put there. Some of it's pain, but beneath that I see hope. And that's the one I'm going to latch onto. "I wouldn't care if you were pregnant or not, Freckles. I'm not walking away this time, are you?"

She blinks, fat tears spilling out and rolling down her cheeks as she seems to process my words. "You want to stay?"

"Yes." I press a kiss to her lips. "If you'll let me. I need you more than I need air, Izzy." Peppering each cheek with a kiss before resting my forehead against hers. "I love you, Izzy. I think deep down, I probably always have."

The door cracks open and the doctor pokes his head in. "Is it safe to come in?"

I smile and whisper, "You ready for some serious conversation, Freckles?" She nods her head, her eyes wide with disbelief. "She's a little shell-shocked, doc. I think she was expecting me to fall over at the news of her pregnancy."

He chuckles, "Well, let's see if my news makes that happen." Izzy and I share a glance. I don't know if he thinks his news is going to trump the fact I'm going to be a dad—it won't because there isn't anything more shocking than that. "Izzy. When you came in last night, we were concerned about your fall and did a sonogram to check the baby as well as an MRI to rule out a head injury since you came in unconscious. And well…"

"Oh my God." Izzy whimpers. "Is there something wrong? Did I hurt the baby? Or did you find a tumor… Fuck—Roland, I knew there was something else going on." She leans into me as I shift in the bed to sit beside her. Pulling her close to my side, I rest her head against my chest.

"Calm down, Freckles. If something was wrong, you wouldn't be sitting here like this." My eyes narrow on the doctor, silently demanding him to confirm my reassurance to her. "Right doc?"

He takes a deep breath and shrugs. "You don't have a tumor—or head injury. Izzy... the reason your body is struggling to keep up is because the pregnancy is taking more than you're providing. But that's to be expected when a petite woman such as yourself is carrying multiples."

"Multiples?" My arm flexes as I tighten my hold on Izzy. "She's pregnant with two—not one?" I turn and look down at the equally shocked woman. "You said *baby*, Izzy. One baby. Not two."

"Yes, twins. And with that comes the need for you to *gain* weight, Miss Holiday — not lose it. You need a higher calorie diet, but that doesn't mean I want to leave here and go get the all-you-can-eat pasta bowl at Olive Garden. You need lean protein and *lots* of dark, colorful veggies. The issues with fatigue, headaches, and weight loss are from you not eating enough... and your iron is dangerously low because what you *are* eating is junk. You're going to have to make some serious changes, Miss Holiday. Skip the cookies and go for more leafy greens. The closer you get to delivery, the more food you're going to need."

"Wait.. how many weeks is she?"

He shoves the file he's holding under his arm and grins. "Almost ten weeks. I imagine you'll start to show more soon enough—for a lot of moms, they go to bed one night and wake up with a baby bump the next morning. I'm going to keep you a little while longer and pump you full of the nutrients you've been lacking. But when you go home, I expect you to stay off your feet as much as possible and eat—a *lot*, Miss Holiday. Your babies need quadruple what they've been getting. You can consider it bed rest until further notice."

The doctor turns, pausing at the door. "The nurse will be in to get some new meds started. If your numbers stay stable and still look good, you might get out of here first thing in the morning, but more likely, it will be afternoon at best. Let me know if you need anything." He pulls the door closed, leaving the nuclear fallout with us to manage.

*Jesus. H. Christ.*

Izzy looks so frail now… I can't imagine what she'll look like when she's carrying a dump truck sized belly in a few months. My swimmers must be fucking super soldiers, because I've never had a close call—not even once. It figures the one time I lose my head and forget to wrap my dick; I knock the woman I love up with a ready-made family. For the first time, I'm thoroughly pissed at my pecker. It's gotten me into more trouble than I can count, but this takes the cake. And worse… it screwed Izzy over, too. I snort, making her glance over and cock an eyebrow.

"What's so funny, Roland? Because I'm not laughing right now. I just got used to the idea of *a* baby and now I'm hearing your fucking spastic sperm put two in me. *Two.* You get that? Two goddamn babies and we haven't even figured out *us.*"

I can't help it, but I bust out laughing at her ragey outburst. Izzy doesn't find my reaction funny and presses both palms into my side, giving me a pretty good shove, so I fall off the bed. I land with a thud onto the cold, hard ass floor. It doesn't stop me, though. I'm in tears by the time I drag myself to my feet. Even funnier is the expression of Liam and Alex, who've opened the door and are staring at me like I've finally lost my mind.

"Um… hope we aren't interrupting, but we saw the doctor, and he said she was awake." Liam glances around the room like being here right now makes him uncomfortable. "Dare I ask why you're on the floor? I mean, you probably deserve it, but can I get a confirmation?"

"Because I pushed him—he's fucking laughing. *Laughing*. This isn't a funny situation, and it's pissing me off. Why don't you get over here and manhandle his stupid ass out of my room? I need a minute alone."

Moving faster than she expects, I lift myself off the floor and lean over the bed, pushing my fingers through her unruly mop of fire and tilt her head back. "No. I let you push me away once. That's not happening again." I slam my mouth over hers, stealing the retort she's about to say. I pour every ounce of feeling into the kiss, so much so she's breathless when I pull away. "I wasn't laughing at you, *Freckles*. I was laughing at the reality of our situation."

"Well... I guess that means she forgave your ass for leaking those photos and making more work for her friend Candice and me.' Alex plops down in the chair. "If everything is hunky-dory, when can we leave?"

I suck in a breath and close my eyes at his slip, one hand balling into a fist at my side as I groan softly.

"What is he talking about, Roland?" Izzy glances over at Alex and growls at him. "What photos, *Alex*?"

"Fuck." Liam grumbles. "You didn't tell her? What the hell Roland. I thought you were going to get it all out in the open—come clean."

Afraid to look at her, I palm my face and mumble from under my hand. "I was going to when I had the *chance*. In the excitement of everything, I kind of forgot to mention something to you."

She grunts, the irritation clear in her body language as she pulls away. "I think you should leave." She flops back on the bed and closes her eyes. "I'm tired."

"Then you can just listen, Izzy. Because I'm not walking out that door until you know every damn thing. You're carrying my babies, so you aren't getting rid of me that easily or *ever* again."

Liam coughs—more like gags. "Did you just say babies?"

Jerking my head in his direction. "Yeah… Izzy and I are having *babies*. Now, if you'll take *big* mouth over there and leave, I'd appreciate some privacy."

Liam grabs Alex by the arm and practically drags him to the door. "You… are going to explain what you mean by 'babies…'" Liam makes air quotes with his hands as he backs out of the room, pulling Alex along like a naughty scamp. "But for now, we'll go back to the cafeteria and wait…let you two work things out…"

"Oh, for fuck's sake." Izzy sits up and fists my shirt, jerking me toward her. "Grow some balls, Roland. You two—" She shoots daggers toward them. "…should probably know that this dumb prick's sperm is made of some kind of superpower swimmers. He didn't just knock me up—he fucking saddled me with a litter. We're having twins. Now, get the hell out."

She flops back again and rolls to her side, facing the wall as I stand there dumbly. Liam's eyes are comically wide as he bumps into Alex and stumbles out of the room. "Holy fuck… Roland's going to have *two* babies? This is epic."

He slams the door closed, muffling his and Alex's laughter, but all I can do is stare at the wooden frame. Izzy's soft voice breaks the trance I'm under. "You should go with them."

"Stop, Izzy. Just hear me out, Ok?" When she doesn't answer I keep talking. "When the incident at the club happened, I thought it would make the label keep you on longer. And when I heard you'd left, I knew it was the wrong decision. But I made another shitty choice by leaking the photos to the tabloids again. I thought you'd come home, but the PR firm cleaned up the mess before you could. I realized then I was going about it all wrong. Not to mention hanging out with my brothers' girlfriends and helping them get better, I realized they had what I wanted—someone to love me like they love my brothers. Drake is a better man because of Rhiannon, and I bet my ass Gage is because of Poppy. When he gets out of prison, anyway. And *that's* because my brothers love these women fiercely."

I press my hand against her back. "Come on Izzy. Tell me you can forgive me and give me a chance to prove I'm not the same guy I was weeks ago. I won't leave you until I know you're going to let me in. Even if it means giving up my career—I'm not walking away from you ever again because *you* are my person. You're the reason my heart is finally beating again."

*Izzy*

I WANT to scream from the mountain tops at his declaration, but I don't. Instead, I lay there, letting him rub my back and replay his words over and over. Can I trust him not to run when things get hard? I don't know, and that scares the ever-loving shit out of me. Not to mention, I'm mad as hell to learn *he*'s the reason I had to spend days threatening lawsuits... but he doesn't know that. Which makes me just as much a liar.

"I lied to you." I whisper the words out into the open.

Roland slides onto the bed and wraps his arm around me. He tugs me back, so I'm nestled in his front. The bed isn't enormous, but somehow it fits us perfectly. "What'dya say, Freckles?" His voice is low and filled with warmth, despite my bitchy attitude earlier.

Roland's fingers brush against the tiny swell housing our babies, making my eyes well with tears. "I said I lied to you."

His hand stops moving for a second and splays across my bump. "What do you mean... you *lied*? About what?"

He probably thinks I mean about him being the father, so I hurry and speak, squashing those possible thoughts. "I didn't quit. I've been managing your publicity from here—not Candice. I couldn't leave your career at the hands of anyone, not even her. I think it was my way of holding on to you even after I ran. I'd messed everything up and in some delusional way, I thought by keeping your image clean it would keep you whole. Music is all you have, Roland." I shift to my back so I can look him in the eyes. "If your career died, I was worried I'd lose you, even though I never really had you."

"Damn, Izzy. That means the photo leak—"

I press my finger to his lips. "Stop… what's done is done. We both made some pretty shitty mistakes handling this. We let fear dictate our lives for too long. And now we have other things to worry about."

"Like my two offspring taking up residence here?" He flattens his palm over my belly and grins. "I know you think this is too much for me—for *us*. You're wrong, though. I want these babies to know what love is, Izzy. I want them to see their parents in love, *real* love, and know that's how it's supposed to be. Not the fucked-up version my brothers, and I got. Oh, *shit*."

"You need to call them." I cut him off, a sigh slipping from my lips. "Gage is home, and I took you away from seeing him." I pinch my lips together to keep from crying. "I'm sorry Roland. You should have been there when Gage got out—not here with me."

"Wrong." He grunts. "I'm right where I'm supposed to be. Let's call them together. They're going to flip their shit."

I watch as he slips off the bed and moves to the corner of the room. He pulls the phone sitting on the window's edge off the charger and climbs back into bed with it in his hand. Roland snuggles up to me, pulling me so I'm half laying on his chest.

"You sure you want to tell them over the phone and not in person?" I trace my fingers over the shirt he's wearing. Beneath the cotton is the tattoo that's been burned into my head since the night I tore his shirt open. "This is a big deal... maybe we should wait until we get home."

He freezes, his body tensing beneath me. "You said home. Does that mean you're going to come back with me, Izzy? Because I was serious when I said I was staying until you do."

Tilting my head up, I peek at him from beneath my eyelashes. "Were you serious about giving this a go? It scares me Roland—to take a chance. But I love you, too. And being alone down here has sucked beyond words. I think I'd rather risk my heart being broken because you can't handle everything, than risk not knowing. So, yes... I want to go home with you... if you'll have me."

Roland drops the phone to the mattress and rolls toward us so that he's partially covering me. His fingers tangle in my hair as he pulls me against his chest and covers my mouth with his. My entire body heats up as his kiss makes promises of what's to come, and I can't help it when I move my leg over his. Roland lets out a growl when I rub myself against his leg, trying to stave off the pressure building.

"Izzy." He breaks the kiss, his eyes roaming over my body. "What are you doing, Freckles?"

"God... Roland, you set my damn body on fire." I bury my head in his chest. "And being pregnant makes it ten times worse."

"Is my poor baby needy?" He strokes my back. "I promise to take care of you when we aren't trapped in a bed at the hospital."

"Ugh." I groan, flopping myself over onto my back. I reach out and cup the bulge in his pants and give his erection a squeeze. Roland covers my hand with his, then grabs my wrist firmly.

"While you know I like that... let's not make me cum in my pants like a sixteen-year-old boy, please. Someone could walk in and see —and no one but me gets to see you like that, Freckles."

"Fine." I jerk my hand back. "Then I want to go home."

Like Roland had a premonition or something, the nurse walks in. She smirks at his position on the bed, and blushes when she scans his body. I have no doubt she'll be telling all her nurse friends about my man's package... seeing as it's hard as a rock right now and trying to bust through the zipper of his jeans.

"Sorry to interrupt, but I need to hook up some new meds. Dr. Vallara has ordered this to help with your calorie intake. You'll get one more after this one and then hopefully go home tomorrow morning. Congratulations, by the way, twins are exciting."

Roland wraps his arm around my waist and lays his head down on my pillow. He presses soft kisses against my temple as she hangs the bag on the pole beside me. She checks my IV and vitals. "Everything is looking up—your vitals are much better tonight. Mine would be too if I had *him* wrapped around me." She jerks her head at Roland.

I smile at her, "Yeah... he's exactly what I needed, I guess."

"You want me to have them bring you in a cot?" She glances at his precarious position next to me. "It'll be more comfortable than trying to squeeze in with her."

He shakes his head no. "Thanks, but I'm not moving. We're fine like this. Can you tell the two guys who were in here earlier—one's big, the other one's ugly... that she's sleeping and not to disturb us? They can come back in the morning."

"Sure thing. I'll try to be quiet when I come in to change out the bag." The nurse heads out, flicking the light switch on her way, leaving the room in mostly darkness.

The only light is the tiny fluorescent strip above the bed. It's just enough glow to see Roland's features as I look at him. "I can't believe this is my life."

"Believe it, baby. And it's *our* life. Let's make that call now. I promised Drake I'd let him know when you woke up… this call is kinda overdue." He laughs as he fishes the phone out of the bed.

"Does he hate me?" I close my eyes and snuggle into his hold. "For leaving you the way I did?"

"Not at all. He knows I'm hard to handle… he doesn't fault you for trying to protect me—even if he doesn't know what it was from." He swipes the screen, basking the room in its bright glow.

"Roland… tell me you have good news." Drake's husky voice fills the hospital room.

Roland squeezes me as he speaks. "She's awake and here now. Izzy, say hi."

"Um… hi."

Drake laughs. "Hang on, Gage is here. I'm going to put you on speaker."

"Roland." Gage's voice washes over us and I feel Roland's sharp intake of breath.

Glancing at his face, I realize he's speechless and fighting back tears. Slipping the phone into my hand, I stretch my body so I can kiss him. "Sorry, Gage. Give him a second."

"Is this the woman who's managed to snag his heart?"

"Yes. We met briefly at the Atlanta concert. I'm so sorry he's here with me and not at home with you, Gage. I was stupid and ran when I should have been honest with him."

"Meh… we Winstons like to do things the hard way. All that matters is he has you now."

Drake butts in. *"Does* he have you now?"

"Yes. Forever, if he'll take me."

Roland chuckles as he wipes the wetness from his face. "Kinda hard to get rid of me now. She's stuck with me for at least eighteen years."

"Eighteen years?" Drake mumbles, "What the hell does that mean?"

"I really didn't want him to tell you like this—over the phone. But he doesn't want to wait."

Gage's voice is filled with mirth as he speaks. "Wait? Roland, you wanna tell us what she's talking about?"

"Well, you two old farts are going to be uncles."

Drake mumbles something and Gage starts laughing. "Holy shit. My little brother knocked up a woman. You mean he's not a virgin?"

"Hardly… and that's not all." I cut in. "It appears your *baby* brother's sperm is made of some bionic matter because not only did he knock me up—he put two inside me."

I kind of wish I could see their faces because the silence is almost comical. "Did you just say *two?*" Gage finally talks. "My brother— the twenty-five year old rockstar, is going to be the father of *two?*"

"Yep." I pop the p, making Roland laugh.

"What can I say, boys… my shit's made of solid gold. Looks like my swimmers are rock stars too, because we're having twins."

I hear a woman speaking in the background through the phone's speaker. "Hang on, Roland, Rhi wants to talk to you."

"Hey Rols… Did I just hear correctly? You're going to be a dad?"

"Yes ma'am. Izzy, say hello to Drake's woman."

"Hi, Rhiannon." I press my cheek into his chest. "Looks like you're going to be an auntie of sorts."

"Please, for the love of God, tell me you two are coming home." She sounds excited, and that makes me feel a relief I didn't know I needed to feel.

Roland gives a look and smiles. "We are. Look, Izzy needs to rest, so I'll call you guys tomorrow when we get released. Glad you're home, Gage. I Love you guys."

"Love you too, Rols."

He disconnects the phone and tosses it to the floor. "You could have broken that." I mumble against his shirt.

"Don't care. I can afford to buy a new one. Let's get some rest… it's been one hell of a day and my babies need to sleep."

Something that's been bothering me tickles the forefront of my mind. "Roland." I shift closer. "Why'd you postpone the concert? And when is it? You haven't missed it because of me, have you?"

Roland twirls my hair around his fingers. "I told the label to push it off or cancel it—it didn't matter to me. With you gone, and then the shit with Gage and Poppy, I just needed to regroup. Music hasn't felt the same since all this went down—nothing has, Izzy. I'm supposed to be in Austin in a few months. But if this life isn't what you want, then I'll walk away from it. Austin can be the end. I won't let my career come between me and my family ever again."

"I don't want you to quit, Roland. Lots of musicians have families."

He presses his hand against me, pulling me even tighter to his frame. "Am I hurting you?"

"No… this is perfect."

"Good." He presses a kiss to the top of my head. "Let's table this discussion for later. Right now, the only thing that matters is you and those babies. Once we know you're in the clear, we'll get home and figure everything out then. Ok?"

This man is more than I expected. Maybe it's true what they say— love can heal the broken. Even if it didn't, I would still love him, broken pieces and all.

"I love you, Rols."

"I love you more, Freckles."

# Roland

THE ROAR of the crowd is deafening as I step out onto the stage. After Izzy got released from the hospital, we wasted no time getting back home. Several long conversations later, we decided she would quit the PR firm and be my personal PR manager. Makes sense, seeing as she owns my heart too. She flew with me to Austin for the make-up concert. Then, the label begged me to do one more to show my fans I wasn't quitting like the rumors were saying. After taking some time with Izzy, I finally agreed—but under two conditions.

One, it had to be here—in Atlanta. And two... I got to take an extended break after.

I agreed to write some new music while on hiatus with my wife, yeah, *wife* and babies. I still can't believe she married me. It took some major begging and a quick flight to Vegas, but that's exactly what happened. Now, at thirty-five weeks, we are counting down to the arrival of the twins once Izzy receives one more steroid shot to strengthen their lungs. Since the pregnancy has been so hard on her, her doctors want the babies Earth-side sooner than later and won't let her go past thirty-seven, though I'm convinced it will be sooner.

At the last scan, we learned one of the two baby's genders. We're having a girl. The other bundle wasn't as cooperative, so we won't know until the little bugger comes out. Izzy is determined to birth them naturally—with drugs, of course, but the doctor here in Atlanta has warned her that her birth plan may not go as she expects with her being induced early, and to be prepared to roll with the punches.

"Hello, Atlanta!" I scream out to the crowd, who go ballistic. "How's everyone doing?" Their roar is like fuel to my soul. I glance back at Izzy, whose smile fills me with such love I have to shake my head. "If you didn't know it already, my wife and I are about to welcome the next generation of Savage Realm."

My band mates jam a riff, creating a flurry of screams and whistles. We burst into the set, playing with so much heart. Even I'm shocked at how well it's going. Izzy hasn't just changed me, she's changed the guys. If I can't get her something, one of them does. Mikey treats her like she's glass and at least once a day she threatens to shove his drum sticks up his ass if he doesn't back off. We've grown into one big ass dysfunctional family.

As we wind down, I take a second and address the crowd. This is something I've been working on for a while and convinced the guys to play it tonight.

"I hope you guys don't mind, but I want to play something new for you. I love you, Izzy… this one's for you, Freckles." I nod toward the guys and strum my guitar.

*This is where we start*

*Twenty miles and poles apart*

*Where worlds collide and days are dark,*

You have my Soul, you have my heart.

Without you I have nothing

You're my strength, my light in the dark

You're all that I believe in, without you there's no joy in me

The truth trapped me there under your weight

I know I'd never be me without your security

Your loving Lips keeping me from harm

Put your hand in my hand, and together we'll stand

This is where we start

Twenty miles and poles apart

Where worlds collide and days are dark

You have my Soul, you have my heart.

I Drowned and Dreamt of having someone like you

So overdue for this feeling so new.

Swept away, caught up in this moment

A beautiful disaster together in love

Your presence is like a shadow on me, and it's all I can see.

I've been alone on this road so many times before

Now I don't have to hide from the world

Because all I needed was someone to help me see it through

This is where we start

Twenty miles and poles apart

Where worlds collide and days are dark

*You have my Soul, you have my heart.*

*This is where we start*

*Twenty miles and poles apart*

*Where worlds collide and days are dark*

*You have my Soul, you have my heart.*

As soon as the song ends, the crowd erupts into shouts of approval. Izzy has tears streaming down her face as she stands off to the side watching. Holding my hand out, I beckon her onto the stage. "Come here, Freckles. Say hi to Atlanta."

I didn't think it was possible, but the crowd gets louder as she wobbles out onto the stage beside me. Izzy tosses her hand up in a wave before pressing it against the ginormous ball of a belly in front of her. "These are my babies, Atlanta! Can you believe this woman made me a dad?"

Leaning into her, I smash my lips over hers and kiss her. "Good night ATL." I call out as I drag her off the stage. "You ready to get out of here?"

"Yes—my fucking feet are killing me. Roland?" She halts my movement. "I can't believe you wrote that for me." Izzy slams her mouth against mine, her tongue shoving against my own. Her belly separates us from getting too close, but the palm of her hand cupping my cock tells me exactly where this is leading. "Take me home."

Hell yeah… sex has gotten kinky as fuck with her pregnant. She's turned out to be the perfect mix of bossy and submissive. And I've learned I like being in control when it comes to *her* pleasure. Izzy has finally given me the balance I need—and shown me how to deal with my pain in a healthier way.

As we make our way down the hallway, Izzy suddenly comes to a stop. I turn to look at her in concern. "Hey you ok?"

"Sorry. I've been having Braxton Hicks today. Nothing major, but they hurt like fuck." I see her wincing through a contraction.

"Maybe we should stop by the hospital and be sure. Doc did say they could come anytime now."

Izzy shakes her head in disagreement. "No. If you take me to the ER, they're going to shove their fingers inside me to check me and I want your cock, not a damn intern's examination."

"Come on Freckles. We need to make sure our daughter, and he or she who shall not be named, are alright." I tug her hand toward the exit. "Then you can have my dick. Jeez... I feel like I'm just some slab of meat for you."

"Yep—and I'm craving sausage. Let's get the hell out of here and not waste time on nothing."

After checking in with my manager and the rest of the band, we find Liam out back. He's waiting for us by the exit door. "Hey momma... How's my niece and nephew doing?"

Liam has dubbed himself our babies' honorary uncle and is convinced the second one is a boy. He's probably right, seeing as the Winston men are stubborn as hell and this little guy or gal wouldn't show any bits for the camera.

"Fine—except this jackass wants to go by the ER to hear I'm only having fake contractions." Liam's eyebrows shoot to his hairline.

"You're having contractions? Ok... get in, let's go." He rushes us to the waiting SUV and helps Izzy inside. "Good call, Rols. We need to make sure everything is fine."

I ease in beside her and wince. "What the fuck, Freckles? Why'd you pinch me?"

She furrows her brows and growls. "Because now you have him ganging up on me. Ow, shit." She grabs at her belly. "And apparently, your spawn, too."

"See… let's just get you checked out. The last thing we need is for us to be fucking and somebody start crowning… I do *not* want to saddle my kid with that kind of entrance into the world."

I tap on the window at Liam, who's standing outside the car on his cell phone. He glances into the car with an expression that makes me suck in a breath. Something is wrong—it's written all over his face. He pockets the phone and climbs inside. "Change of plans. We're going to the ER, but not for Izzy."

"What do you mean, not for Izzy? Liam… start talking right now."

Izzy clutches my hand in hers and squeezes, grounding me like she knows I need it. "That was Drake. It's Gage, Roland. He was in a car accident, and they rushed him to the emergency room."

"What the hell was he doing out at this time of night, for fuck's sake?"

Liam backs us out of the parking space and navigates the car onto the busy streets without an answer. My concert is letting out, which means a five-minute ride to the hospital will take more like twenty.

"I don't know. Drake said Poppy called him in hysterics. He and Rhiannon are meeting her at the hospital. This is so fucked up."

"Uh oh." Izzy's soft voice penetrates the haze and I glance over at her.

"What is it, Freckles?"

She closes her eyes and takes a deep breath. "Maybe you were right —I don't think they're pretend contractions."

My eyes widen and flick to Liam when the car jerks suddenly. "Why'd you say that?"

She winces, her fingers tightening around mine. I press my hand against her belly and gasp. "Holy shit, her stomach is like a diamond. Why's it so hard, Izzy?"

"Because..." she tries to take a deep breath, but gasps instead. "I'm having a contraction—and it's definitely a real one." Her eyes well with tears.

I press a kiss to her head. "I thought you said it was Braxton Hicks?"

"It's not." She pants, her eyes squeezing shut as she tries to breathe through this one. "It's definitely not."

Liam glances over his shoulder. "We're almost there. You sure this is the real deal, Izzy?"

Her eyes pin me with a sorrowful glare, and she nods, biting down on her lip. "Yeah... *positive*."

"Fuck." I grumble. "Liam... pull into the ER sallyport. Get us close to the door."

Izzy growls beside me. "I'm sorry, Rols. You can just drop me off at the entrance and Liam can take me."

"What the fuck, baby? That's not going to happen, and I can do both. Liam is taking us to the hospital Gage is at. We can deal with both... uh...situations..." I press her belly, relieved it's not nearly as hard as before. Pulling her hand in mine, I press my lips to the top of her hand. "It's ok. This is a good thing, Freckles. We're going to meet our babies. Liam can go check on Gage while we welcome them into the world. Nothing else matters."

The car stops in front of the entrance and Liam jumps out. As soon as he pulls open the door, I slide out and help Izzy to her feet. "This is it, baby. This is the moment we've been waiting for—Gage will be fine. I'm sure of it. He has to be. He survived the mob, for fuck's sake." Wrapping my arm around her, I help her waddle into the ER. "Let's go meet our daughter and learn what baby two is. Then we can worry about the others."

Drake is standing at the counter on his phone. His eyes widen when he sees Izzy. "Whoa, little brother. Looks like coming here was the plan, anyway."

"Yeah—she's in labor. How's Gage?"

Drake smiles. "He's going to be fine. A drunk hit him going through an intersection and totaled his car. He's got a broken leg and is in surgery getting it repaired."

Izzy winces as the nurse seats her in a wheelchair. "Roland." She groans, bending over as she clutches her belly. She shifts in the seat, pressing her hands between her legs and pulls it out to hold it up. Shimmering in the soft glow of the hospital lights, I can see her fingers are coated in a wet substance.

"My fucking water just broke."

"Go, Roland. Take care of her. I'll let Rhi and Poppy know you're here and what's happening. This is a good thing—new babies will be a happy addition to the family."

"Love you, Bro." I give him a quick hug as I follow beside Izzy. "What do you need, Freckles?"

"For you to never touch me with that monster dick again...Oh my *God*." She cries out. "This is awful. I hate you, Roland."

"No, you don't... you love me and you're about to make me even happier than I was." We're wheeled into a labor room and the nurse helps her onto the bed. I watch as they help her strip out of her dress and slip her into a hospital gown. Her face is flush from the contractions, but despite the pain she's in, Izzy wears a smile.

She grabs my hand like it's in a vise and pulls me toward her. "You're right… I love you, Roland." Her lips press against mine and it takes everything in me to pull away. "Guess this means I'm not getting your cock tonight. Probably best… it's what got us in this mess, anyway."

*Drake*

THIS IS SUPPOSED to be a happy moment—my baby brother is adding two new additions to our family… but all I'm feeling is anxiety. And that's from the letter I've got clenched in my hand, buried in my pocket.

I'd just opened the damn thing when I got the call about Gage, leaving me with no time to process what I was reading. Stepping out of Gage's room, I pull the folded paper out and open it. The words aren't foreign to me. I've seen these plenty in my line of work. But not like this—not when my family is at the receiving end.

"What's wrong, Drake?" Rhiannon's voice washes over me and I turn to find her watching me. "And don't tell me it's nothing. I can see it written all over your face right now and I'm betting it's got something to do with that letter in your hand."

I ball up the paper and sigh. "How is it you can read me so easily, little Dove?"

"That's how it works when you really love someone. Now fess up… you should be happy. Gage is going to be alright, albeit he's going to need time to heal, but it could have been worse. A *lot* worse. And

Roland is about to make you an uncle twice over. That's something to celebrate. Yet, I find you out here pacing the hallway."

"I got this today—a court processor delivered it to my office."

She shakes her head, "And? You're an attorney, Drake. Isn't that the daily norm?"

I don't want to tell her because when I do, it will be confirming my father was truly a bastard. More than any of us actually knew. This letter is going to stir up a whirlwind of shit none of us are ready for. Unfurling the crumpled mess, I hand it over to Rhiannon. Her eyes grow wide as she reads the words printed right there in black and white.

"Oh, my God. Is this for real?"

"'Fraid so." I take the letter back and shove it into my pocket. "Please keep this between us for now. At least until I meet with the other attorney."

Rhiannon steps into my arms, wrapping her own around my waist. "This is like something out of a movie—you think your dad might have another family?"

"With that monster, anything's possible. He wasn't a nice man and was gone a *lot*. But this is going to change our lives and at the worst possible moment. This should be about my baby brother and the lives he's bringing into the world with Izzy. Not some fucked up family secret."

I take a deep breath, trying to calm the nerves bubbling inside my chest. "I've lived my whole life knowing my brothers, and I had to work twice as hard to get out from beneath the stench of my father. He wasn't a nice man or husband—and an even worse father. This is like the cherry on a shit life."

Rhiannon shifts to look up at me. "You know what else this means?"

I shrug against her hold, pressing a soft kiss to her head. "Aside from the fact my dad was an abusive asshole to *multiple* women?"

"It means there's more Winstons out there."

Her words are like a torpedo to my gut. She's right—this letter means far worse than I gave it credit for. It means the two bundles of joy being born as I stand out here and stew aren't the only new Winstons.

No… *this* letter means there are other monsters out there we never even knew about.

The secrets and lies of the Winston family go deeper than even Drake can imagine.
Faith will be shaken, darkness will be found, and passion will rule.
Grab the next shocker in Bad Blows (Book 4)
Releasing 2023

# AVAILABLE

## Books

Visit www.authordoripulitano.com or
scan the QR code for more books.

# ABOUT

## Dori Pulitno

*"Welcome to the dark side. We have sexy Mafiosos."*

Dori P is the naughtier, much dirtier half of USA Today Bestselling author, LC Taylor. The bad girl Dori embraces her Italian side with heroic hitmen, decadent conflicted dons, and oh so f*ckable assassins trying to trade their devilish ways for salvation and the perfect woman to tie to their bed.

And F**k following the rules… this author is most definitely trigger happy.

Sign up for Dori's newsletter and never miss a new release.
www.authordoripulitano.com